FOR CENTURIES, THE CHINESE WERE CON-
SIDERED MASTERS OF REFINED SADISM.

They looked upon torture as art. Its practitioners
were honored men in an esteemed profession.
Frequent exhibits—to which the public was invited—
were held to demonstrate new inventions or further
grotesque refinements.

In the great city of Canton, they built an elabo-
rately beautiful garden. In the midst of its perfumed
flowers, the most horrifying of tortures, carried out
with the most fiendish of instruments, took place.

Octave Mirbeau used this historically real, socially
terrifying background for this novel. His main character, a young French civil servant, is lured into using
pain for pleasure by the woman he loves. She cannot
experience sensual excitement without the trappings
of terror.

Written at the turn of the century, THE GARDEN
OF EVIL has been published, from time to time, in
English-speaking countries under the titles of "The
Garden of Tortures" and "The Pleasure Garden."

To the priests, to the soldiers, to the judges, and to the men
who educate, lead and govern mankind
I dedicate
these pages of murder and blood.

O.M.

This edition published 1973 by
David Bruce and Watson Ltd.
44 Great Russell Street London WC1
SBN 85127 011 5
Printed in Holland by
Holland Printing Partners / Krips Repro Meppel

THE GARDEN OF EVIL

Octave Mirbeau

Translated by Raymond Rudorff

David Bruce & Watson
London

PART ONE

MY MISSION

BEFORE I relate one of the most frightful episodes of my travels in the Far East, it might be of interest if I briefly explain the circumstances in which I was led to undertake this voyage. It's part of contemporary history.

To those who might be astonished by the anonymity I have jealously preserved in the course of this judicial and painful narrative, I shall say: "Never mind my name! ... It is the name of someone who brought much suffering to others and to himself—even more to himself than to others —and who, after many upheavals, and after having one day descended to the depths of human desire, is trying to recover his soul in solitude and obscurity. Peace to the ashes of his sin."

I

Twelve years ago, no longer knowing what to do and condemned by a series of misfortunes to the harsh necessity of either hanging myself or throwing myself in the Seine, I presented myself as a candidate in the general elections— my last resource—in a department where I knew no one and had never set foot before.

It is true that my candidacy had been officially supported by the cabinet which no longer knew what to do with me and thus found an ingenious and delicate way of freeing itself once and for all from my daily, harassing solicitations.

On this occasion, I had a solemn and familiar interview with the minister who was my friend and an old school friend.

"You see how nice we are to you!" said this powerful, generous friend. "We've hardly saved you from the clutches of the law—and we were hard put to it—and now we're going to make a member of parliament out of you."

"I'm still not nominated," I said in a peevish tone.

"No doubt! . . . But you've got every chance . . . You're intelligent, charming, prodigal, a good boy when you want to be and you've got the sovereign gift of being able to please . . . A lady's man, my dear fellow, is always the man of the crowd . . . I'll answer for you . . . What you must do is to understand the situation well . . . Anyway it's very simple . . ."

And he warned me :

"Above all, no politics! . . . Don't involve yourself . . . don't get carried away! In the constituency I've chosen for you there's one question which dominates all the others : that of the beetroot . . . The rest doesn't count and only concerns the prefect . . . You're a purely agricultural candidate . . . even better, exclusively a beetroot growing one . . . Don't forget it . . . Whatever may happen in the course of the fight, stay firm as a rock on this excellent platform . . . Do you know anything about beetroots? . . ."

"My word, no!" I replied. "I only know that sugar and alcohol are made from it . . . everybody knows that!"

"Bravo! That's enough," the minister said applaudingly, with a reassuring and cordial air of authority. "Go straight ahead on that basis . . . Promise fabulous returns . . . extraordinary and free chemical fertilisers . . . railways, canals and roads for the transport of this interesting and patriotic vegetable . . . Announce reductions in taxes, premiums for growers, fierce duties on competing products . . . anything you like! . . . In this matter you've got *carte blanche* and I'll help you . . . But don't get carried away by personal or

6

general polemics which might become dangerous for you and, with your election, compromise the prestige of the Republic . . . Because, between ourselves, old fellow—I'm not reproaching you with anything, I'm simply observing —you've got a rather awkward past . . ."

I wasn't in the mood for laughing . . . Vexed by this remark which seemed both useless and unkindly, I replied sharply, looking full in the face of my friend who could read all the accumulated, clear-cut, cold menaces in my eyes :

"You could more rightly say 'we have a past'. It seems to me, dear friend, that your own can hardly envy anything in mine . . ."

"Oh, me! . . ." said the minister with an air of superior detachment and comfortable insouciance, "it's not the same thing . . . As for me, dear friend, I'm covered—by France !"

And going back to my election, he added :

"Therefore, I resume . . . Beetroots, more beetroots, always beetroots ! . . . That's your programme . . . Take care not to get away from it."

Then he discreetly handed me some funds and wished me the best of luck.

I faithfully followed the programme which my powerful friend had outlined for me and I was wrong . . . I wasn't elected. As for the crushing majority which fell to my opponent, I attribute it, apart from some disloyal manoeuvrings, to the fact that that devil of a man was even more ignorant than I and even more notoriously villainous.

Let us remark, *en passant,* that in the age we live in, a well-displayed villainy takes the place of all the finer qualities and the more infamous a man, the more people are disposed to credit him with intellectual force and moral worth.

7

My opponent, who is now one of the least controvertible illustrations of what politics are, had often stolen on many occasions in his life. And his superiority stemmed from the fact that far from hiding the fact he boasted of it with the most revolting cynicism.

"I've stolen . . . I've stolen . . ." he would shout in the village streets, in the town squares, along the roads, in the fields . . .

"I've stolen . . . I've stolen," he would proclaim in his confessions of faith, his posters and confidential circulars . . .

And in wine-shops, his agents would sit perched on barrels stained with wine and filled with alcohol, and repeatedly trumpet these magic words: "He's stolen . . . he's stolen . . ."

Wonderstruck, the laborious populations of the towns and the valiant populations of the countrysides would acclaim this bold man with a frenzy that increased day by day, in direct proportion to the frenzy of his avowals.

How could I fight against such a rival who possessed such advantages, I whose conscience was only burdened by such youthful peccadilloes—which I modestly dissimulated—as household thefts, ransoms of mistresses, cheating at cards, blackmail, anonymous letters, informing and forgeries? Oh, the candour of ignorant youth!

One evening, at a public meeting, I was almost beaten unconscious by electors who were furious because, in view of the scandalous declarations of my opponent, I had proclaimed not only the supremacy of the beetroot but the right to virtue, morality and probity, and the need to cleanse the Republic of all the individual stains dishonouring it. They rushed at me; they seized me by the throat; I was lifted up and flung around like a parcel, pummelled by the fists as I was passed from hand to hand . . . By good luck I only paid for my rush of eloquence with a bruised cheek, three bruised ribs and six broken teeth . . .

8

This was all I earned in this disastrous enterprise in which I had so unfortunately been involved by the protection of a minister who called himself my friend.

I was beside myself.

I was even more justified in my fury by the fact that, just as the battle was at its thickest, the government abandoned me, leaving me without support with only my beetroots as an amulet with which to come to an agreement and treat with my opponent.

Although he had been very humble at first, the prefect soon became very insolent; he refused me the information necessary for my campaign; lastly, he shut—or practically shut—his door in my face. The minister himself no longer replied to my letters, gave me nothing I had asked for, and the newspapers devoted to him directed underhand attacks against me, and made wounding allusions under the cover of polished, flowery prose. They didn't go as far as to fight me officially but it was clear to everybody that I'd been dropped . . . Oh, I don't believe so much spleen ever went into a man's soul!

On my return to Paris, firmly resolved to make an outburst at all costs, I demanded explanations from the minister. My attitude immediately made him accommodating and pliant.

"My dear fellow," he said, "I'm so sorry for everything that's happened to you . . . Upon my word I am! You see me as sorry as could be. But what could I do? . . . I'm not the only one in the cabinet and . . ."

"You're the only one I know!" I interrupted him violently, making a pile of files jump on his table as I banged my fist on it. "The others aren't my concern . . . There's only you . . . You betrayed me . . . it's ignoble!"

I strode up and down the office uttering threats and banging the chairs.

"So you had a good laugh at my expense! Let's see who laughs last! At last the country will know what a minister's like! You fool, don't you know that I hold you, your fortune, your wealth, all your secrets in my hands? So my past bothers you, does it? Well, just wait then! Tomorrow—yes, tomorrow—it'll all be out!"

I was choking with rage. The minister tried to calm me, took me by the arm and gently drew me towards the armchair out of which I had just leapt.

"Please listen and be quiet!" he said in an imploring tone. "Please listen, I beg you! Sit down, now! Listen this is what happened . . ."

Very quickly, in short, jerky sentences, he began :

"We didn't know your rival . . . He showed himself in the fight to be a very strong man—a statesman even! You know how short we are of ministerial material. Even though the same old faces keep coming back we occasionally need a new face to show the Chamber and the country. Now there just aren't any—can you think of any you know? Well then, we thought that your rival might be one of those new faces. He's got all the qualities suitable for a provisional or crisis minister. Anyway, as he could be bought—do you see? . . . It's too bad for you, I agree. But the country's interests come first . . ."

"Don't be silly, we aren't in the Chamber here. It's not a question of the country's interests for which you don't give a damn—nor me either . . . It's a matter of myself. Now, thanks to you I'm down and out. Yesterday afternoon the cashier at my bank rudely refused me a loan of only twenty francs. My creditors had counted on my winning and are furious, they're after my skin . . . Today I haven't even the price of a meal. Do you think we can leave it at that? Are you that stupid—as stupid as a member of the majority?"

The minister smiled, tapped me on the knee familiarly and said :

"If only you'll let me speak. I'm quite prepared to offer you compensation . . ."

"Re-pa-ra-tion!"

"All right, reparation!"

"In full?"

"In full! Come back in a few days. No doubt I'll be able to offer it to you myself. In the meantime, here's a hundred *louis*. It's all I've got left from the secret funds."

He gently added, with a note of cordial good humour :

"Another half dozen lads like you and there'd be no budget left!"

Such liberality was more than I had expected and had the effect of calming me for the instant. I pocketed the two notes he handed me, smiling—not without grumbling since I did not wish to show myself either disarmed or satisfied—and retired with dignity.

As for the three days that followed—I spent them in the vilest debauchery . . .

II

Let it be permitted to me to go back again in time. Perhaps it is not unimportant that I should say who I am and where I came from . . . The irony of my destiny will thus be better explained.

I was born into a family of the lower bourgeoisie—that staunch, thrifty and virtuous lower bourgeoisie which—so official speeches tell us—is the backbone of France. Well, well—I'm not any the prouder for it !

My father sold wheat. He was a rough and ready man with a wonderful flair for business. He had the reputation of being very clever in business and his great cleverness consisted in "getting the better of people" as he put it. To cheat over the quality of his merchandise and its weight, to get two francs for what he had bought at two centimes and, whenever he could get away with it, to sell the same thing twice over, such were his principles.

For example, he would never deliver grain without first soaking it in water so that the swollen grains would weigh twice as much—especially when a little fine gravel was added, an operation that my father practised conscientiously. After all, nothing must be wasted in business and everything counts. My mother who was even more avid for ill-earned profit, helped him in his ingenious depredations and would mount guard over the cash-box, stiff and distrustful like a soldier mounting guard before the enemy's lines.

A strict Republican, a fiery patriot—he also sold to the army—an intolerant moralist and, in the popular sense of the word, an "honest man", my father showed no pity for the dishonesty of others, especially when it affected him personally. He never tired of speaking of the necessity for honour and virtue and one of his favourite precepts was at the same time the synthesis of my education at home :

"To take something from someone and keep it for oneself—that's theft. But to take something from someone and pass it on to someone else in exchange for as much money as you can get, that's business . . ."

It was in just such a moral atmosphere that I grew to manhood, alone as it were, with no other guide than the daily example provided for me by my parents. From the age of ten I had no other philosophy of life than that of theft and I was firmly convinced—oh! quite ingenuously, I assure you—that to "get the better of people" was t e sole basis for all social relationships.

It was my school that determined the bizarre and tortuous twist to my existence for it was there that I met the boy who was later to become my friend, the famous minister Eugene Mortain.

He was the son of a wine merchant and had been trained to politics, as I had been to trade, by his father, who was the main electoral agent in the region, a vice-president of this, a founder of that, a leader of professional unions and groups, etc., with the result that since childhood Eugene showed himself to have the soul of a "veritable statesman".

Although he was a scholarship pupil he immediately won us over by his obvious superiority in effrontery and indelicacy and also in his solemn, empty phraseology which succeeded in whipping up our enthusiasms. Moreover, he had inherited his father's highly profitable and all-conquering mania for organisation. In a few weeks, he had soon transformed the school playground into all kinds of associations and sub-associations, committees and sub-committees in which he had himself elected president, secretary and treasurer, all in one. He founded associations of football players, top-spinners, leapfrog jumpers and heaven knows what else and every member of these various associations was obliged to pay into the central fund—my friend's pockets—a monthly subscription of five *sous* which also counted as subscription for the newspaper that Eugene Mortain edited to propagandise ideas and defend the interests of what he called "autonomous and comradely" groups.

Evil inclinations and appetites common to us both immediately drew us together and our close relationship became a keen, continuous exploitation of our comrades who were so proud to become members of all these groups. I soon became aware that I was the weaker accomplice but, by virtue of this very realisation, I held on all the more firmly to my ambitious friend's fortunes. Although I might not get an equal share, I was at least assured of some crumbs . . . They were enough for me then. But alas, all I ever had were those crumbs from the cake that my friend was devouring!

I met Eugene again, later, at a difficult and painful time in my life. By dint of "getting the better of people" my father brought about his own downfall. A delivery of grain which seemed to have poisoned an entire barracks crowned the total ruin of our house which had been founded in 1794. My father might have been able to survive dishonour, for he knew the infinite capacity for indulgence of our age, but he could not survive ruin. An attack of apoplexy carried him off one evening, and he left my mother and I without a penny.

No longer being able to count on him, I was obliged to fend for myself. Tearing myself away from my mother's lamentations, I ran to Paris where Eugene Mortain welcomed me royally.

He was gradually rising in the world. Thanks to his skilful exploitation of parliamentary patronage, the sublety of his nature and his absolute lack of scruples, he was beginning to be mentioned favourably in the world of the press, of politics and of finance. At once he employed me in his dirty work and by living constantly in his shadow it was not long before I acquired part of his notoriety, although I was unable to profit from it as I should have done. But I have always lacked the ability to persevere in evil. Not that I have any latent pangs of conscience, remorse, or fleeting urges for honesty : some diabolical perversity in me forces me, without any apparent reason, to lose control of the best-conducted affairs, and to loosen my grip on the firmest-held throats. I have practical qualities of the first order, a very keen sense of life, an audacious way of attempting and proposing the impossible and succeeding in it, but I lack the necessary tenacity of a man of action.

But, with an eye to the future and feeling that the fatal day would come when my friend Eugene would want to be rid of me, since I ceaselessly represented an embarrassing past in his eyes, I was clever enough to compromise him in scandalous incidents and far-seeing enough to keep undeniable proof of them. At the risk of falling from favour, Eugene had to drag me after him perpetually, as though I were a cannon-ball fastened to his leg.

Before reaching the Chamber of Deputies, Eugene Mortain had tried his hand at every branch—even the lowest—of journalism. As he was devoured by pressing needs and ruinous appetites, there was no important piece of blackmail or disreputable affair in which my good friend Eugene was not in some way the mysterious moving spirit. By a stroke of sheer genius he had syndicated a large part of the press in order to carry out his operations successfully but he was modest enough not to boast of his *coups* and he had the precious art of knowing how to use other people and never expose his own person to risks. He showed never-failing skill and a perfect knowledge of his chosen domain for intrigue by always avoiding the snares and pitfalls of the law although it is true that my aid was far from unimportant to him on many occasions.

Such then was the man in whom I had placed my last hopes and who held my life and my death in his hands.

It will be noticed that in this brief outline of my friend, I have modestly effaced myself even though I made a powerful and often curious contribution to his fortune. I could tell you many stories which, as you may be sure, are far from edifying. But what use is a complete confession since you can divine all my turpitudes without my having to give any further details? And then, my role as accomplice to this daring but cautious scoundrel was— oh! certainly not insignificant—always more or less a secret one. But sometimes, by a strange quirk of honesty, the idea of being taken for his "man of straw" repelled me and I would even lose sight of him for months on end. Sometimes, in a fit of poetic fervour, I would go and lose myself in the depths of the countryside and there, face to face with nature, I would aspire to a life of purity, of silence and moral recovery which, alas, never lasted! And I would go back to Eugene, at times of crisis. He always welcomed me with the cordiality I expected of him. It was plain that he would certainly have liked to be rid of me but

15

I would sharply remind him of the truth of our mutual situation.

One day, I distinctly saw the flame of murder shine in his eyes. I was by no means worried for I clumsily put my hand on his shoulder, like a policeman collaring a thief, and mockingly said :

"And then what? What good would it do you? Even my corpse would accuse you. Don't be so silly! I've let you get where you wanted . . . I've never foiled you in your ambitions . . . On the contrary, I've worked for you loyally . . . as best as I could . . . loyally . . . haven't I? Do you think I enjoy seeing you strutting in the limelight while I stupidly wallow in the mud below? And yet, for a mere trifle, I can send that marvellous fortune of yours that we both built up so laboriously—"

"Oh! Both of us?"

Eugene whistled.

"Yes! The two of us! For a mere trifle I could send it crashing down. I've only to say the word, and you'll fall from power into the convicts' yard—from being the minister that you are to being the convict that you should be if there was any justice left and if I wasn't the worst of cowards . . . Anyway, I won't say that word . . . I'll let you go on enjoying the admiration and esteem of great men and foreign courts since, you see, I find it wonderfully funny! Only, I want my share, do you understand, my share?"

Eugene then gave an embarrassed smile and said :

"But you're mad to tell me all this! And what's the use? Have I ever refused you anything, you old buffoon?"

With a wealth of grimaces and gestures that amazed me, he added gaily :

"Would you like the cross of the Legion of Honour, for instance?"

Oh, he was a charming fellow all right!

A few days after the violent scene that followed my lamentable failure, I met Eugene in the house of a friend, at Madame G***'s where we had both been invited to dinner. We shook hands cordially. No one would have said that there had ever been any ill-feeling between us.

"We no longer see you," he said with that tone of indifferent friendliness which, for him, was none other than the politeness of hatred. "Were you ill?"

"Not at all . . . simply on the way to forgetfulness."

"Quite. By the way, have you calmed down now? I'd like to talk to you for five minutes after dinner."

"Have you any news?" I asked with an evil smile to show him that I wasn't going to let him get rid of me afterwards as though I were an affair of no account.

"Me?" he said, "No . . . nothing . . . just a plan . . . anyway, we'll see . . ."

Why had I decided to go to Madame G***'s that very evening? I really don't know for I was very depressed and in no mood for amusement. My anger against Eugene had died down—for the time being at least. In its stead, an immense weariness and an immense disgust filled me. A disgust with myself, with the others, with everybody . . . Since the morning I had been seriously reflecting on my situation and despite the minister's promises—which I had no intention of letting him forget—I could see no suitable way out for myself. I realised that it would be very difficult for my friend to procure me any official, stable, honourably parasitical or administratively remunerative position which would enable me to finish my days in peace as a respectable old man or as an official enjoying a sinecure's living. In the first place, even if I had had such a position, I would probably have wasted it at once. And then, my being given such a position would have aroused a storm of protests on every side in the name of public morality and republican virtue, and questions would have been asked which the minister would not have been able to answer. All he could offer me were a few miserable financial expedients for postponing the inevitable hour of my downfall. And even then I could not count eternally on this minimum of favour and protection since Eugene himself could not go on relying on the eternal stupidity of the public.

To work at bringing about the downfall of my comrade, to skilfully insinuate myself into the graces of some potential new ministerial leader, to regain my social virginity by collaborating with some new leader—I had thought of it all. But I no longer had the courage to begin again. I had burned the candle of my youth at both ends. I was weary of these precarious and perilous adventures which had led me—where? . . .

As he was besieged on all sides, it was not until very late that Eugene was able to join me. We took advantage of the fact that a famous singer was monopolising the general attention for a moment to take refuge in a sort of little smoking-room, discreetly lit by a long, slender lamp shaded in pink crêpe. The minister sat on a divan, and lit a cigarette while I casually sat backwards on a chair and folded my arms. He spoke with gravity :

"I've been thinking of you a lot these past few days."

He nodded his head.

"Yes, I've been thinking about you a lot. You don't believe me? Yes, I can see that you don't believe me. You're thinking that I'm only thinking of making a fool of you like the others. That's it, isn't it? Well, you're wrong, my dear fellow. But if this meeting bores you, nothing's easier than to end it."

"All right ! I'm listening."

Eugene smiled.

"All right then. Don't sulk. Listen to me. I've thought

18

a lot . . . You must go away. In your own interests, for your own future, it's the only solution I've found. Let's see now! Are you—how shall I say it—are you an embryologist?"

He read my answer in the look of panic that I threw him.

"No, you're not an embryologist. A pity! A great pity!"

"What are you asking me that for? What kind of a joke is this?"

"The fact is that at this moment I could have some considerable credits—relatively considerable anyway—for a scientific mission which it would give me pleasure to entrust to you."

And without giving me time to answer, he explained the whole affair to me in a few short, comical sentences accompanied with buffoon-like gestures :

"It's a matter of going to India or Ceylon, I think, to explore the seas . . . in the gulfs . . . To study what scientists call pelasgic jelly . . . Do you understand? And to hunt among gasteropods, corals and what-have-you for the primordal cell of life . . . the protoplasmic beginnings of organised life, do you see? Anyway, it's something like that. It's charming and, as you can see, very simple."

"Very simple," I murmured automatically.

"Ah, but you're not an embryologist," this veritable statesman concluded.

And with benevolent sympathy he added :

"What a nuisance!"

My protector reflected for a few minutes. I remained silent, not having had the time to get over my astonishment at such an unexpected proposition.

Eugene began to laugh with discreet malice.

"There's always the secret police . . . Perhaps we could find you a good vacancy there? What do you say?"

In a difficult situation, my mental faculties become stimulated, my energy increases tenfold, and I am gifted with an ability to suddenly change my mind and make a new and prompt decision which always surprises me and which has often served me well.

"Done!" I cried. "After all, I might as well be an embryologist for once in my life. What am I risking? Science won't suffer for it! Agreed! I accept the mission to Ceylon."

"And you're quite right," said the minister. "Bravo! Especially as embryology, Darwin, Haeckel and all that, must be simply an enormous joke! Ah, my boy, you won't be bored there. Ceylon is marvellous. It seems there are extraordinary women there—of such beauty, such temperament ... It's an earthly paradise! Come to the ministry tomorrow. We'll arrange it all officially. And in the meantime, don't go shouting about it all over the roof tops because, as you know, I'm playing a dangerous game which can cost me dearly. Let's go now!"

The evening that had begun in sadness ended in joy.

My preparations were soon over. My mission promised favourably. By an exceptional circumvention of bureaucratic procedure, it was only a week after this decisive meeting in the house of Madame G*** that I obtained the above-mentioned credits without any trouble or delay. They were liberally calculated, unlike the poor little budgets granted to real scientists. No doubt I owed this unusual liberality to the fact that I was not a real scientist, and thus needed even greater resources to be able to play the role.

They had budgeted for two secretaries and two servants, the highly expensive purchase of anatomical instruments, microscopes, photographic equipment, folding canoes, diving bells and even glass flasks for scientific collections, hunting rifles and cages for bringing captured animals back alive. Really, the government was doing things handsomely and I had nothing but praise for it! I need hardly say that I bought none of these *impedimenta* and that I decided to travel alone, counting on my own ingenuity to lead me through the unknown jungles of India and science.

I took advantage of my leisure to learn about Ceylon, its customs and landscapes, and to get an idea of the life I would be leading there in the terrible Tropics. Even discounting exaggerations and boastings and the lies in travellers' tales, what I read enchanted me—particularly one detail reported by a serious German scientist, It appeared that there was a marvellous villa or bungalow set amid the fairy-like gardens of the suburbs of Colombo, in which a rich and eccentric Englishman kept a kind of harem containing perfect physical examples of the women of every Indian race. I promised myself that I would find some way of getting introduced to this amateur polygamist and confine my studies of comparative embryology to his harem.

The minister responsible for my mission approved all my arrangements and gaily praised my virtue of thrift. As for that other minister, that scoundrel Eugene, he could hardly contain his emotion. There was true enthusiasm in his eyes and a sincere trembling in his voice. Two small tears came running down his eyes. He shook my hand so hard he nearly broke it. For a few minutes, the two of us were the unconscious and comical dupes of our own mystifications.

Ah! When I think of it!

Provided with letters of introduction to the "authorities" in Ceylon, I finally embarked on the *Saghalien* one fine afternoon at Marseilles.

No sooner had I set foot on the steamer than I was at once convinced of the effectiveness of an official title and realised how, thanks to its prestige, a ruined man, as I was at the time, could grow in the esteem of strangers and passers-by and, consequently, in his own eyes. The captain who "knew of my admirable work" overwhelmed me with attentions and honours. Both the most comfortable cabin and the best place at table had been reserved for me. As the news had soon spread among the passengers that an illustrious scientist was on board everyone took the utmost pains in showing their respect for me . . . On every face I saw nothing but blossoming admiration. Even the women showed signs of curiosity and goodwill, some more discreetly, others more daringly. One above all violently aroused my curiosity. She was a marvellous creature with thick red hair and green eyes flecked with gold, like those of a wild animal. She was travelling accompanied by three chambermaids one of whom was Chinese. I asked the captain about her.

"She's English," he said. "They call her Miss Clara . . . The most extraordinary woman you could imagine . . . Even though she's only twenty-eight she already knows the entire globe . . . At the moment she's living in China . . . It's the fourth time I've had her on board . . ."

"Rich?"

"Oh, very rich . . . Her father died a long time ago and was, they say, an opium merchant at Canton. That's where she was born. I think she's a bit cracked but charming."

"Married?"

"No . . ."

"And . . . ?"

In this one word I put a whole wealth of intimate and even lewd meanings.

The captain smiled.

"As for that . . . I don't know . . . I don't believe so . . . I've never noticed anything—here."

Such was the reply of the good captain who, on the contrary, seemed to me to know a lot more than he would tell. I didn't press the point but I told myself in my usual elliptical way:

"You, my girl—you're just right for me !"

At that time I would have been quite incapable of the slightest poetic description since poetry only came to me later, with love. Certainly, like everybody else I enjoyed the beauties of nature but they didn't excite me to the point of swooning. I enjoyed them in my manner which was that of a moderate Republican. And I told myself :

"Nature, as seen from a train window or a ship's porthole, resembles herself always and everywhere. Her main characteristic is that she lacks the unexpected. She repeats herself constantly, having only a small quantity of forms, combinations and aspects which one finds again here and there, all more or less the same. In her immense and burdensome monotony, she only differs in nuances which are hardly perceptible and of no interest except to flea-trainers which I am not, even though I may be an embryologist, and hair-splitters . . . To sum up : when you've travelled through a hundred square miles of country— anywhere—you've seen it all. And to think that scum Eugene was yelling : "You'll see the country there . . . those trees ! those flowers !" Trees get on my nerves and I can only stand flowers in dress-shops or on hats . . . As far as tropical nature goes, Monte Carlo would have been quite sufficient for my aesthetic landscape-lover's needs and for my dreams of far-off travel. I only understand palm-trees, coconut trees, banana trees, mangroves, grape-fruit trees and pines if I can pick up some nice little number, some pretty little woman chewing something other than betel nuts between her teeth . . . Coco-palms, cocottes rather—my idea of trees is a thoroughly Parisian one . . .

Oh the blind, deaf brute I was then ! How could I have displayed such heart-rending cynicism in blaspheming against the infinite beauty of the Form which goes from man to the beast, from the beast to the plant, from the

23

plant to the mountain, from the mountain to the cloud, and from the cloud to the pebble whose reflection contains all the splendours of life itself?

Although it was October the crossing of the Red Sea was a very painful process. The heat was so crushing and the air so heavy to our European lungs that I often thought that I would die of suffocation. In the daytime we never left the saloon where the great Indian *punka* flapped without cease, giving us the short-lived illusion of a fresh breeze, and we spent the nights on the deck where it was no more possible to sleep than in our cabins. Among the passengers, those who had shown themselves to be the most boastful or intrepid had all collapsed, limbs inert and throats wheezing, like foundered horses. Nothing was more ridiculous than the sight of these people slumping in their multi-coloured pyjamas. Only the two Chinamen on board seemed unaffected by this furnace-like temp-erature. They had changed neither their ways nor their clothes and passed the time either by silently promenading on the decks or by playing cards or dice in their cabins.

We were interested in nothing. In any case, there was nothing to take our minds off the torment of feeling our-selves broiled with all the slowness and regularity of a *pot à feu*. The steamer was sailing in the middle of the gulf: above and around us there was nothing but the blue of the sky and the blue of the sea, a dark blue, a blue of heated metal which here and there reflected the glow of a furnace on its surface. We could scarcely see the Somali coast, it appeared a remote, red vaporised mass of moun-tains of burning sand where not a tree, not a blade of grass grew and which, like an ever burning brazier, closed in on this sinister sea so like an enormous reservoir of boiling water.

I must say that during this crossing I showed great courage and succeeded in showing nothing of my real state of suffering. This I managed through fatuity and love.

Hazard—was it hazard or the captain?—had given me Miss Clara for my neighbour at table. A slight incident when the meal was served enabled us to become acquainted almost immediately. Moreover, my lofty scientific rank and the curiosity I had aroused gave me exemption from the ordinary conventions of polite behaviour.

As the captain had told me, Miss Clara was going back to China after having divided her summer between England for her interests, Germany for her wealth, and France for her pleasure. She confided to me that Europe disgusted her more and more. She could no longer stand its constricting ways, its ridiculous customs and its chilly landscapes . . . She only felt happy and free in China! With her very decisive manner, her very exceptional way of life, her way of sometimes talking at random and sometimes with a lively feeling for things, her feverish gaiety with a bent for the strange, the sentimental and the philosophical, the impure and the candid, the mysterious, with her omissions and evasions, her incomprehensible whims and her terrible determinations, she greatly intrigued me even though I knew one can expect anything from the eccentricity of an Englishwoman. But I had no doubt from the very start that I, who as far as women were concerned, had never met any but Parisian cocottes and—what is worse—political and literary women, would easily get the better of her and I promised myself that I would enliven my trip with her in a manner both unexpected and charming. With her red hair, her shining skin, a laugh always ready to burst forth from her full red lips, she truly was the joy of the ship and, like the soul of that vessel, on her way towards the wild adventures and Eden-like freedom of the virgin forests and burning tropics . . . The Eve of some marvellous paradise, the flower of her own being, the flower of wild intoxication and the savoury fruit of eternal desire, I could see her wandering and leap-

25

ing among the flowers and golden fruits of some primordial orchard and not in her modern white spotted suit that so well displayed her slender waist and the powerful swell of her bust, but in the supernaturalised splendour of all her Biblical nudity.

It was not long before I recognised the error of my amorous diagnosis and realised that, unlike what I had hoped for in all my vanity, Miss Clara was of an impregnable virtue. But far from being dismayed by such a realisation, she only appeared all the prettier to me and it gave me veritable pride to think that, pure and virtuous as she was, she had welcomed one as ignoble and debauched as myself with such simple and gracious trustfulness. I did not wish to hear my inner voice which cried out to me : "This woman is lying . . . this woman is making fun of you . . . Just look, you fool, at those eyes of hers which have seen everything, that mouth that's kissed everything, those hands that have caressed everything, that flesh which has so often quivered with every pleasure and in every known embrace! Pure is she? And those knowing gestures? And that softness and suppleness and that way of bending the body that has known every embrace? And that swollen bust swollen like some flower pod drunk with pollen? . . ."

No, to tell the truth, I didn't listen . . . I felt a delicious sensation, compounded of tenderness, gratitude and pride, a feeling of moral reconquest as each day I advanced still further into familiarity with such a beautiful and virtuous person who, I told myself, would never be anything more for me than a soul! . . . The idea comforted and rehabilitated me in my own eyes. Thanks to this pure, daily contact, I was winning, yes—I was winning back my own self-esteem! All the mud of my past was becoming transformed into a radiant azure blue and I contemplated the future through the tranquil, limpid emerald hue of a regular happiness . . . Oh! How far removed were Eugene

Mortain, Madame G*** and all their kind from me! ...
How all these grimacing phantasms were melting away
with every minute that passed under the celestial gaze of
this lustrous creature through whom I was revealing my
own self to myself as a new man with generosities, tender-
nesses and aspirations I had never known before.

Oh the irony of love's tenderness! Oh the comedy of
the enthusiasms of the human soul! Often, when I was
with Clara, I would believe in the reality and the grandeur
of my mission and believe that I had in myself a genius
that would revolutionise all the embryologies of all the
planets in the Universe ...

We soon got to the point of exchanging confidences ...
By means of a series of cleverly measured lies due on one
hand to my vanity and on the other to the natural desire
not to depreciate myself in the eyes of my friend, I showed
myself to best advantage in my role as a scientist, relating
my biological discoveries, my academic successes, and all
the hopes that the most illustrious men of science had
placed in my methods and my voyage. Then, after leaving
these somewhat arduous heights, I mingled anecdotes of
wordly life with literary and artistic appreciations which
were half-healthy, half-perverse—just enough to interest
a woman without disturbing her. And all these
frivolous and light conversations which I endeavoured
to make as witty as possible gave my serious scientific
personality a particular and perhaps unique character.
I completed my conquest of Miss Clara during the crossing
of the Red Sea. Overcoming my own malaise, I was able
to offer her ingenious remedies and delicate attentions
which soothed her own sufferings. When the *Saghalien*
dropped anchor at Aden to take in coal, she and I were
the best of friends—friends by virtue of that miraculous
friendship untroubled by not the slightest look, and whose
beautiful purity is unsullied by the slightest ambiguous
gesture or guilty intention ... And even so, my inner voice

27

continued to cry out : "But just look at those nostrils of hers, inhaling the whole of life with such terrible voluptuousness. Look at those teeth which have bitten into the blood-stained fruit of sin so many times!" Heroically, I stifled such voices.

It was with an immense joy that we entered the Indian Ocean. After the deadly, torturing days we had spent in the Red Sea it was like a resurrection. A new life, a life of gaiety and activity blossomed on board. Although the weather was still very hot, the air was delightful to breathe, like the odour of a fur that a woman had just let fall from her shoulders. A slight breeze which one would have said was perfumed with all the flora of the Tropics refreshed both my body and soul. Everything around us was dazzling. The sky, as translucent as a fairy grotto, was a golden green, streaked with pink flames; the calm sea, pulsating with a powerful rhythm under the breath of the monsoon, stretched away on all sides as blue as could be, furled here and there with scroll-like waves. We felt, like a lover's touch, the approach of magic continents, and light-filled countries in which life, one mysterious day, had first burst into flower. And every face reflected some of this sky, some of this sea and some of this light.

It goes without saying that Miss Clara attracted and greatly excited men; she was always the centre of a court of passionate worshippers. I was in no way jealous, being certain that she found them ridiculous and that she preferred me to all the others, even to the two Chinese with whom she would often talk but whom she would never look at as she would look at me, with that strange look in which, despite so much reserve, I had several times thought to have detected I know not what secret complicities . . . Among her most fervent admirers were a French explorer who was going to the Malayan peninsular to study the copper mines there, and an English officer whom we had taken on board at Aden and who was going back to his post at Bombay. Each in his own way was a thick-headed but highly amusing oaf, and Clara liked to make fun of them. The explorer never tired of recounting his recent travels through Central Africa. As for the artillery officer, he tried to impress us by describing all his ballistic inventions.

One evening, after dinner, we had all gathered on deck around Clara who was reclining deliciously on a rocking chair. Some of us were smoking cigarettes and the others were dreaming. All of us, in our hearts, had the same desire for Clara and all of us, with the same thought of ardent possession, were following the see-saw motion of two little feet, clad in two little pink mules which were peeping forth from the perfumed petals of her petticoats like the pistils of flowers as the chair rocked back and forth . . . We said nothing . . . The night was wonderfully soft and the boat was sliding voluptuously over the silken sea. Clara suddenly spoke to the explorer :

"Well then?" she said maliciously, "so it's not a joke? You've eaten human flesh?"

"Certainly I have !" he answered proudly with a tone that established his undisputable superiority over the rest of us. "We had to. You eat what you can get . . ."

"And what was the taste like?" she asked, slightly disgusted.

He reflected for an instant and then made a vague gesture :

"My God !" he said, "how can I explain it? Look, my adorable little lady, just imagine pork after it's been somewhat marinated in nut oil . . ."

With a resigned tone he casually added :

"It's not very nice . . . Anyway, you don't eat it out of gourmandise . . . I prefer a leg of lamb or a steak . . ."

"Obviously !" agreed Clara.

And as though she wished, out of politeness, to diminish the horror of this cannibalism, she added :

29

"No doubt because you only eat Negroes' flesh?"

"Negroes?" he cried, with a start, "Pooh! Happily, my dear lady I was never reduced to that harsh necessity. We were never short of whites, God be thanked! Our escort was a large one and mostly made up of Europeans, Marseillais, Germans, Italians, a bit of everything ... When we were starving we shot down one of the escort—preferably a German. The German, my divine little lady, is fatter than the other races and he provides more meat. And then, for we French, it's always one German less! The Italian is dry and hard ... He's full of nerves ..."

"And the man from Marseilles?" I asked him.

"Pah!" went the man, shaking his head. "He smells of garlic ... He's edible but that's all ...".

He turned again to Clara and with protesting gestures he went on :

"But a Negro—never! I believe I would have vomited. I know people who've eaten Negroes. They all fell ill. The Negro isn't edible. Some, I assure you, are even poisonous."

But he scrupulously corrected himself :

"But after all, one has to know them well like mushrooms. Perhaps the Negroes in India let themselves be eaten?"

"No!" declared the English officer with a sharp, categorical tone thus bringing this culinary discussion, which was beginning to make me feel sick, to an end in the midst of a burst of laughter.

Somewhat disconcerted, the explorer resumed :

"Never mind ... despite all these little worries I'm very happy to be going back again. In Europe I'm a sick man ... I'm not alive ... I don't know where to go ... I find myself degraded and imprisoned in Europe, like a wild beast in a cage ... Impossible to find elbow room, to stretch your arms or to open your mouth without coming up against stupid prejudices and idiotic laws ... and iniquitous customs ... Last year, my dear Miss Clara, I was walking in a corn field. I was knocking down the corn sheaves around me with a cane to amuse myself . . . I've the right to do as I like, haven't I? A peasant came running up, shouting and insulting me, telling me to get out of his field . . . You've no idea what he was like! What would you have done in my place? I gave him three good blows with my cane on his head. He fell with a cracked skull . . . Well now, guess what happened to me?"

"You ate him perhaps" Clara laughingly insinuated.

"No, they dragged me before I know not how many judges who sentenced me to two months in prison and ten thousand francs for damages . . . For a filthy peasant! Is that what you call civilisation? Would you believe it? Not for me thanks! Just think what it would have been like if I'd been given the same sentence in Africa every time I killed a Negro or even a white man!"

"So you also kill Negroes?" asked Clara.

"Certainly, my pretty lady!"

"But why, if you don't eat them?"

"But to civilise them which is to say to take their hoards of ivory and rubber . . . And then, what do you expect? If the governments and commercial firms who entrust us with these civilising missions were to learn that we haven't killed anybody—what would they say?"

"But why should you kill them?" I objected for I felt myself becoming good-hearted and full of pity.

"But I told you—to civilise them. And it's very amusing! When after a long, long march we would get to a Negro village they would all be so frightened! All at once they would start crying out and would be so frightened that instead of trying to flee they would fling themselves down and start to cry. We gave them spirits for we always carried large stocks of alcohol in our provisions and then, when they were drunk we would shoot them down!"

The night passed in its dazzling splendour; the sea was on fire; all around us great sheets of phosphorescent light

31

floated on the waves . . . I was sad, sad for longing for Clara, sad for these coarse men and for myself, and sad because of these words which offended both silence and Beauty!

I had the feeling that for the last few minutes the captain had been trying to speak. He took advantage of the pause that followed this confession:

"I've done much better than all that," he said. "Your little massacres are nothing compared to those which will be attributed to me. I've invented a bullet which is quite extraordinary. And I've called it the Dum-Dum bullet after the name of the little Hindu village where I had the honour of inventing it."

"Does it kill many people? More than the others?" asked Clara.

"Oh, my dear Lady, I can't tell you how many!" he said laughingly. "You can't count how many!"

But he modestly added:

"And yet, it's nothing . . . it's tiny! Just imagine something no bigger than a hazel nut . . . It's charming!"

"And what a pretty name, Captain!" said Clara admiringly.

"Very pretty indeed" agreed the captain who was visibly flattered "Very poetical!"

"You might say, mightn't you, that it was the name of a fairy in a play by Shakespeare. The fairy Dum-Dum—I find that enchanting . . . A laughing fairy, light and graceful and fair-headed, leaping, dancing and running in the heather in the sunshine! And there she goes, little Dum-Dum!"

"And there she goes!" repeated the officer. "She goes very well, dear lady. And what I believe to be unique is that with her there aren't any more wounded to speak of."

"Ah!"

"Only the dead! That's what is so exquisite about her!"

32

He abruptly went on to another reverie :'

"I sometimes ask myself if it's not a tale by Edgar Allan Poe or a daydream by Thomas de Quincey . . . But no—since I've tried out this lovely little Dum-Dum myself . . . I'll tell you the story . . . I got hold of twelve Hindus and placed them—"

"Alive?"

"Naturally! The Emperor of Germany conducts his own ballistic experiments on corpses but you must admit that it's absurd and quite unsatisfactory . . . I myself use people who aren't only alive but also in perfect health and with robust constitutions. At least you can see what you're doing and where you're going . . . I'm no dreamer—I'm a scientist!"

"I beg your pardon, Captain. Please go on."

"Well then—I placed twelve Hindus one behind the other in a geometrically straight line and then I fired . . ."

"And then?" interrupted Clara.

"And then, my delightful little lady, the marvellous little Dum-Dum worked wonders. Of twelve Hindus not one remained standing! The bullet had gone through their twelve bodies which were afterwards no more than twelve heaps of mangled flesh and literally crushed bone . . . It was really like magic! I would never have believed I'd be so wonderfully successful . . ."

After a few seconds of moving silence he dreamily reflected :

"I'm looking," he murmured confidentially, "I'm looking for something better . . . something more final . . . I'm looking for a bullet—a little bullet which would leave nothing of anyone it hit . . . nothing . . . nothing . . . nothing . . . Do you understand me?"

"How? What do you mean by nothing?"

"Oh, very little!" the officer explained, "barely a heap of ashes, or even just a slight reddish cloud of smoke which would dissipate at once . . . It could be done!"

After he had calmed down again he said:

"I can see the day when after learning of this splendid device, France will not insult us again in all her newspapers. And it will be the fiercest of your patriots, those who are always shouting the loudest that enough millions are never spent on warfare, and who always talk of nothing but killing and bombarding, who will once more hold up England to the execration of all civilised peoples . . . But my God! We're only being logical in our state of universal barbarity . . . What? You agree that shells should explode and then you don't want bullets to be the same? Why not? We live under the law of war and what does war consist of? It consists in massacring as many men as possible in the shortest time possible. To make war even more murderous and destructive we must find even more destructive devices . . . It's a question of humanity and also of modern progress . . ."

"But captain," I objected, "and the rights of peoples? What would you do about that?"

The officer laughed and raised his arms to the sky:

"The rights of peoples," he replied, "it's the right we have to massacre people *en masse* or singly, with shells or bullets—it doesn't matter with which as long as people are duly massacred!"

One of the Chinese spoke:

"But we're not savages!"

"Not savages? And what are we then, I beg you? We're worse savages than those in Australia since even though we are aware of our savagery we persist in it. And then, since it's by war, which is to say by theft, pillage and massacre, that we mean to govern, trade, settle our disputes and avenge our honour—well then, all we have to do is to accept the disadvantages of this state of brutality in which we still wish to keep ourselves . . . We are brutes—very well! Let's act like brutes!"

Then Clara said in a deep and gentle voice:

34

"And then, it would be sacrilege to fight against death. Death is so beautiful!"

She rose to her feet, white and mysterious under the electric lights on the deck. The fine, long silken shawl that covered her seemed to envelop her with pale, changing reflections.

"Until tomorrow!" she said.

We all clustered hurriedly around her. The officer had taken her hand and was kissing it and I hated his masculine face, his thin waist, his high-strung movements and his forceful gait . . . He apologised :

"Forgive me for letting myself be carried away by such a subject and for forgetting that with a woman like yourself one should speak of nothing but love . . ."

Clara replied :

"But, Captain, when you talk of death you are also talking of love!"

She took my arm and I led her back to her cabin where her women were waiting for her, to help her disrobe for the night.

The whole night I was haunted with dreams of massacre and destruction. My sleep was far from tranquil . . . Above the red heather, among the rays of a blood-stained sun I saw her pass, fair and laughing . . . the little fairy Dum-Dum . . . the little fairy Dum-Dum with the eyes, the mouth and all the unknown and unveiled flesh of Clara . . .

My lady friend and I were leaning together over the rails, looking at the sea and looking at the sky. The day was drawing to an end. In the sky, great birds, blue halcyons, were following the ship's course and swaying gently with the exquisite grace of dancing girls; on the water, shoals of flying fish leaped out as we approached and, glittering in the sunlight, descended again only to leap up again and skim over a sea that was a brilliant turquoise blue that day . . . And then shoals of jelly-fish, red medusae, green medusae, purple, pink and mauve medusae and sprays of flowers floated by on the smooth waters. So magnificent were their colours that at each instant Clara uttered yet another cry of admiration as she showed them to me. Suddenly, she asked me :

"Tell me—what is the name of those marvellous creatures?"

I might have invented some bizarre name or found some scientific term. But I didn't even try ... Impelled by a sudden, spontaneous and violent need for frankness I replied :

"I don't know !"

I felt that I was lost and that I was losing all this vague but charming dream which had nourished my hopes and soothed my anxieties for ever . . . that I was falling even lower ... falling back again into the inevitable mud of my pariah-like existence . . . I felt all of this but still there was in myself something that was stronger than myself and which was ordering me to cleanse myself of my impostures, my lies and this abuse of confidence by which I had so basely and criminally stolen the friendship of a being who had had faith in my words.

"No, the truth is that I don't know !" I repeated, giving this denial of mine a tone of exalted drama that it hardly seemed to merit.

"How strangely you say that ! Are you mad? What's the matter with you?" said Clara, astonished by my tone of voice and the strange incoherence of my gestures.

"I don't know ... I don't know !"

And to emphasise my "I don't know !" I violently banged on the rail.

"What do you mean, you don't know? You, a scientist, a naturalist?"

"I'm not a scientist, Clara . . . I'm not a naturalist . . . I'm nothing," I cried. "A wretch ! Yes, a wretch ! I've lied to you ... hatefully ... You must know what kind of man

36

I am ... Listen ..."

Panting and wildly I told her of my life, of Eugène Mortain and Madame G***, of the imposture of my mission, of all my dishonesties and all the mud in my life. I derived an atrocious joy from accusing myself, from making myself even viler, lower and blacker than I really was ... When I had finished this painful recital I told her in a burst of tears :

"Now, it's all over! You're going to hate me and despise me, like the others ... You're going to turn away from me in disgust ... And you'll be quite right ... I won't complain ... It's frightful! But I couldn't go on any longer like this ... I no longer wanted this lie between you and me ..."

I was crying and stammering disjointed words, like a child :

"It's awful! It's frightful! And I who ... who ... it's true, I swear it! ... I was in a trap ... a trap ... I didn't know ... and your soul ... your sweet soul and your pure look ... and the way you welcomed me ... it was my salvation ... my redemption ... my ... my ... It's frightful ... I've lost it all ..."

While I was speaking and weeping, Clara was staring at me. Oh, that look of hers! Never, never will I forget the way that adorable woman was looking at me ... an extraordinary look in which there was astonishment combined with joy, with pity and with love—yes love—as well as malice and irony ... and everything else ... a look which pierced me, penetrated me, searched within me, and overwhelmed both my soul and my body.

"Well, well!" she said simply, "I'm not too surprised. I really do believe that all scientists are like you."

Still looking at me, she laughed prettily :

"I've known one. He was a naturalist of your kind ... He had been sent by the English government to study coffee plant parasites in the plantations of Ceylon. Well, for three months he never left Colombo. He spent all his

37

time playing poker and getting drunk on champagne."

And with her eyes still on me, with that strange, deep and voluptuous look of hers, she paused for a few seconds and then added, in a tone of pity in which I thought I could detect all the delights of forgiveness :

"Oh you little scum !"

I no longer knew what to say or whether I should laugh or cry or even kneel at her feet. Timidly, I stammered :

"Then you don't hate me? You don't despise me? You forgive me?"

"Fool !" she said, "oh, you little fool !"

"Clara ! Clara ! Is it possible?" I cried out, almost fainting with happiness. As the dinner-bell had rung a long time ago and as there was nobody on this part of the deck any more, I moved so close to Clara that I could feel her hips quivering against mine and the heaving of her bosom. And seizing her hands which she let me hold, with my heart beating violently, I cried out :

"Clara ! Clara ! Do you love me? I beg you, do you love me?"

She feebly replied :

"I'll tell you this evening . . . in my cabin !"

I saw a flash in her eyes of a green flame, a terrible flame which frightened me . . . She disengaged her hands from mine and with a hard furrow of her brow, and her head bent, she fell silent and looked at the sea . . .

What was she thinking of? I had no idea. And as I also looked at the sea I thought :

"As long as I was an honest man to her she did not love me or desire me. But from the moment she realised what I am and breathed in the true, impure odour of my soul, love came into her—for she does love me . . . Well, well ! Nothing counts then except evil !"

Evening came and then night fell, without any twilight. There was an indescribable softness in the air. The ship was sailing through a seething mass of phosphorescent foam and great patches of light skimmed over the waters. You would have said that fairies were rising out of the sea, trailing their long mantles of fire and throwing great handfuls of golden pearls into the deep . . .

One morning, as I came on to the deck, I could see, thanks to the clearness of the air, the enchanted isle of Ceylon, that green and red isle crowned by the fairy-like pink and white of Adam's Peak, as clearly as if I had been standing on its soil. The evening before, its approach had been heralded by new perfumes arising from the sea and by a mysterious invasion of butterflies which had suddenly disappeared after having accompanied the ship for a few hours. With no other thoughts in our minds, Clara and I found it charming that the island should have been sending us a message of welcome with these brilliant coloured, poetic messengers. I had reached such a point of sentimental lyricism that the mere sight of a butterfly was enough to send me into a trance of tenderness and ecstasy.

But that morning, the real sight of Ceylon brought me anguish, and even more than anguish, terror. What I saw beyond the waters was not a territory, not a port nor the ardent curiosity evoked by the raising of the veil from the unknown but a brutal recall to my evil life, a return to my former instincts, and the bitter, painful awakening of all that had lain dormant in me and which I had thought dead during our voyage ! It was something more painful than anything I had ever dreamed of and something which it was impossible for me not only to understand but even to conceive in its impossible reality : the end of my wonderful dream which had been Clara's love for me. For the first time, a woman was holding, me. I was her slave. I only wanted her, I wanted none but her and, apart from her and outside her, nothing existed for me. Instead of extinguishing the fires of my love, the fact of possession every day only made the flames burn more fiercely. Each time I advanced even further into the burning pit of her desire and each day I knew that my whole life would be spent in a vain attempt to reach its depths! How could I envisage the prospect of leaving her irrevocable, indissoluble, torturing love for ever, after my soul, my body and my mind had been conquered by it? Madness! This love was as much a part of me as my own flesh; it had taken the place of my blood and the marrow of my bones; it possessed me entirely; it was my entire self! To be separated from her would be to be separated from myself; it would be to kill myself. Even worse! It would be an absurd nightmare : my head in Ceylon while my feet were in China, separated the one from the other by abysses of ocean while I persisted in living in two pieces which were no longer joined together! Could it be possible that the next day, even, I would no longer see before me her swooning rapture and her devouring lips, and that at night I would no longer enjoy the miracle, ever more unexpected, of that divinely shaped body of hers with its savage embraces, and that after long spasms as powerful as crime and as profound as death, I would no longer hear her ingenious little stammerings, her little cries, her little bursts of laughter, her little sobs and her little snatches of song ... I would be losing everything, that which was more necessary for me to breathe than my lungs, for me to think than my brain, for my veins to be nourished with warm blood than my heart even! I belonged to Clara as coal belongs to the fire which devours and consumes it ... To her and to myself, the idea of separation seemed so inconceivable, so madly chimerical and so totally contrary to the laws of nature and life that we had never spoken of it ... Only the night before our two mingled souls had been dreaming, with no need of words, of nothing but the eternity of our voyage as though the ship that bore us was to carry us for ever and for ever, never touching port since to arrive anywhere was to die!

And yet, here was I about to land and bury myself in

that land of green and red, to disappear into the unknown, more terribly alone than ever!

The sea was gentle, calm and radiant. It exhaled a scent of flowery banks and lovers' beds that brought tears to my eyes.

Clara joined me a moment later. Was it because she had loved too much or because she had been crying too much that her eyelids were swollen and her blue-rimmed eyes filled with such great sadness? But there was more in her eyes than sadness : to tell the truth, there was a burning pity, both combative and compassionate. Under her heavy gold and brown hair, a shadow fell across her forehead—that shadow she had in voluptuousness as in pain ... A strangely intoxicating perfume wafted from her hair ... She simply said one word :

"Already?"

"Alas!" I sighed.

She finished adjusting her hat, a little sailor's hat which she fastened with a long gold pin. Her upraised arms made her bust swell so that I could see the line of her sculpted form under her white blouse . . . She continued in a voice that shook slightly :

"Have you thought about it?"

"No!"

Clara bit her lips and sent the blood rushing to them :

"Well then?"

I did not reply . . . I didn't have the strength to reply. My head empty and my heart torn I wanted to slip into oblivion. She was moved and very pale except for her mouth which seemed to me to be even redder and more heavy with kisses. For a long time her eyes questioned me with their heavy, fixed stare.

"The boat puts into port for two days at Colombo and then it leaves again . . . Did you know?"

"Yes!"

"And then?"

"And then . . . it's all over!"

"Can I do anything for you?"

"Nothing . . . thank you . . . it's all over!"

Stifling my sobs in the back of my throat I stammered :

"You have been everything to me . . . more than everything! I beg you, please don't say any more! It's too painful . . . too useless and painful . . . now that it's all over!"

"Nothing is ever over," said Clara firmly, "nothing—not
even death!"

A bell rang. Oh that bell! How it tolled in my heart!

The passengers rushed on deck and among the tumult,
indifferent and reflective, with their hands crossed in their
wide sleeves, the two Chinamen continued their slow,
solemn daily promenade like two abbés reciting their
breviaries.

"We've arrived!"

Already, in the distance I could see pink sails and a
little flotilla of boats moving towards the steamer. The
two funnels were disgorging a mass of black smoke, cover-
ing the sea with a shadow of mourning while the siren
wailed . . . and wailed . . .

Nobody was paying any attention to us. With a tone of
imperious tenderness, Clara asked me :

"Well! what's going to become of you?"

"I don't know! What does it matter? I was lost . . . I
met you. You held me back from the edge of the pit for a
few days and now I'm falling back into it . . . It was inevitable!"

"Inevitable! Why! You're a child! And you've no
confidence in me. Do you think then it was by chance
that you met me?"

After a silence she added :

"It's so simple! I've got powerful friends in China. I'm
sure they could do a lot for you! Would you like me to—"

I didn't give her time to finish :

"No, not that!" I protested weakly. "Above all, not that!

42

I know what you mean . . . don't say anything more."

"You're a child," Clara repeated, "and, my darling heart, you talk as though you were in Europe. And you have the same stupid scruples as in Europe. In China, life is free, happy, complete, without conventions, prejudices or laws—for us at any rate! There are no other limits to freedom than your own self . . . no other limits to love than the triumphant variety of desire . . . Europe and all its hypocritical and barbarous civilisation is a lie. What else do you do there except to lie, to lie to yourself and to others, to lie to everything which, in the depth of your hearts you know to be the truth? You are obliged to feign an outward respect for persons and institutions that you find absurd. You remain timidly attached to moral or social conventions which you despise and condemn and which you know have no justification at all . . . It's the permanent contradiction between your ideas, your desires and all the dead forms and vain semblances of your civilisation which makes you sad, troubled and unbalanced . . . In this unbearable conflict you lose all your joy of life and all feeling of personality because at every minute the free play of your instincts is being constricted, impeded, stopped . . . That's the poisonous, deadly scourge of the civilised world . . . Here it's quite different . . . You'll see! At Canton I have a palace where everything is designed for a life of freedom and love, among marvellous gardens . . . What are you afraid of? What are you leaving? Who will worry about you? When you will no longer love me or when you'll feel too unhappy, you'll go away!"

"Clara . . . Clara!" I implored her.

She stamped her foot on the deck.

"You still don't know me," she said, "you don't know who I am and already you want to leave me! Is it that I frighten you? Is it that you're a coward?"

"Without you I can't live any longer! All I can do is die without you!"

43

"Well then, don't tremble any more . . . stop crying and come with me!"

The green of her eyes was lit with a flash. In a lower, almost harsh voice she said :

"I'll teach you terrible things . . . divine things . . . at last you'll know what love is! I promise you that with me you'll descend to the depths of the mystery of love—and death!"

And with a red smile that sent a shiver down my spine she added :

"Poor child! You thought you were a great debauchee, a great rebel! Oh, all that poor remorse of yours, do you remember it? But your soul is even more timid than a small child's!"

It was true! It was all very well my boasting of being an intransigent scoundrel and believing myself to be above all moral scruples but I would still listen at times to the voices of duty and honour which, at certain moments of nervous depression, would arise from the murky depths of my conscience. The honour of whom? Whose duty? What a pit of folly is man's mind! And in what way was my honour—my honour!—compromised? In what way would I be deserting my duty if, instead of going to Ceylon, I continued my voyage as far as China? Had I really become in my imagination enough of a scientist to believe that I was actually going to "study pelasgic jelly" or to "discover the cell of life" by diving into the sea of the Ceylonese coast? The burlesque idea of taking my embryologist's mission seriously soon brought me back to the realities of my situation. What! Good fortune, a miracle, had made me meet a divinely beautiful, rich and exceptional woman whom I loved and who was offering me an extraordinary life crammed with enjoyments and unique sensations, libertine adventures, sumptuous patronage, salvation and even more than salvation—joy! And was I going to let it all escape me? Once again, was the imp of perversity, that stupid

44

demon—to the stupid obedience of which I owed all my misfortunes—to intervene and advise me to resist hypocritically against an unhoped-for event—a fairy-tale-like miracle—which I would never find again and which I had always hoped for? No! It was really too silly!

"You're right," I told Clara, making my amorous subjugation the sole justification for a submission which also satisfied all my instincts of idleness and debauchery, "you're right . . . I wouldn't be worthy of your eyes, your mouth, your soul . . . of all that heaven and hell which is you, if I hesitated any longer. And then, I couldn't lose you . . . anything rather than that . . . You're right . . . I'm yours . . . take me where you will . . . whether I suffer or die doesn't matter since you—you who I still don't know—are my destiny!"

"Oh, you child! you child! you child!" said Clara in a singular tone the true meaning of which I could not tell, nor whether it was one of joy, irony or pity!

Then, almost maternally, she advised me :

"Now, don't worry about anything but being happy . . . Just stay there and look at this marvellous island. I'm going to settle your new situation on the ship with the purser."

"Clara—"

"Don't be afraid. I know what to say."

And as I was about to offer an objection :

"Shush! Aren't you my child, dear little heart? You must obey me. And then, you don't know . . ."

She vanished, mingling with the crowd of passengers on the deck carrying their suitcases and hand baggage.

Clara and I decided that we would spend the two days in which we were to remain in Colombo by visiting the town and its environs where my mistress had once stayed and which she knew thoroughly. The heat was torrid—so torrid that even the coolest spots—by comparison—in this

45

atrocious country where scientists have situated the Earthly Paradise, such as the gardens by the shore, seemed to be stifling furnaces. Most of our fellow travellers on board did not dare face this fiery temperature which took away the slightest desire to go out and even the vaguest wish to move. I can still see them, ridiculous and plaintive, in the great foyer of the hotel, their heads covered with damp, steaming handkerchiefs—an elegant apparel which they renewed every quarter of an hour and which transformed man's noblest part into a chimney stack crowned with its cloud of steam. Reclining on rocking chairs under the *punka* with their brains liquefying and their lungs choking, they would drink iced beverages brought by boys whose skin colour and bodily structure reminded me of the gingerbread men of my Parisian childhood while other boys of similar aspect would chase away mosquitoes with great blows of their fans.

As for myself, I soon recovered all my high spirits—a little too soon perhaps—and even all my boastful panache. My scruples had vanished and rid of my worries I again became the man I had been when I had left Marseilles : the stupid, bantering Parisian "who can't be taken in" and the boulevardier "who won't let himself be fooled" and who knows how to treat nature—even in the Tropics !

Colombo seemed to me to be a deadly boring and ridiculous town, without anything picturesque and without mystery. It was half Protestant and half Buddhist, as dull as a bonze and as sulky as a pastor and with what joy I inwardly congratulated myself on having miraculously escaped the profound boredom of its straight streets, its motionless sky and its harsh vegetation ! ... It was in vain I searched for the voluptuous women, the Negresses skilled in the practices of love and those saucy little seamstresses that that liar Eugene Mortain had told me about, with his eyes gleaming so meanfully ... And my heart bled for the poor scientists who had been sent here with the problematic mission of conquering the secret of life.

But I realised that Clara did not have any taste for these facile and coarse jests of mine and I thought it prudent to refrain from them, wishing neither to wound her feelings in her fervent worship of nature nor to diminish myself in her eyes. On several occasions I had noticed that she was listening to me with a painful astonishment.

"Why are you so cheerful?" she had asked me, "I don't like to see you so cheerful, my dear little heart . . . It pains me . . . When you're cheerful it means you don't love me . . . Love is something solemn, sad and profound . . ." .

But this still did not prevent her from bursting into laughter at the slightest pretext or without any pretext at all . . . It was thus that she encouraged me in a hoax which I had conceived and which was as follows :

Among the letters of introduction that I had brought with me from Paris there was one for a certain Sir Oscar Terwick who, apart from other scientific titles, was the president at Colombo of the Association of tropical embryology and British entomology. At the hotel where I was staying, I had learned that Sir Oscar was a man of importance, the author of several famous works and, in a word, a very great scientist. I resolved to go and see him. Such a visit could no longer be dangerous for me and then the prospect of meeting a real embryologist did not displease me. He lived a distance away in a suburb called Kolpetty which is, so to speak, the fashionable quarter of Colombo. Clara wished to come with me. She waited for me in the carriage, not far from the scientist's house, in a little square under the shade of immense teak trees.

Sir Oscar received me politely—no more.

He was a very tall, very thin man; very dry, very red-faced and with a square-trimmed beard which came down as far as his navel. He was wearing wide yellow silk trousers and his hairy torso was wrapped in a kind of shawl of pale linen. He gravely read the letter I handed him and after examining me out of the corner of his eye with a distrustful air—was he mistrustful of himself or me?—he asked me in execrable French :

"You are an embryologist?"

I nodded.

"*All right!*" he yapped.

And making the gesture of trailing a net in the sea he went on :

"Embryologist? You? Like this ... in the sea ... *fish* ... *fish* ... *little fish?*"

"Little fish, perfectly ..." I repeated, making the same imitative gesture.

"In the sea?"

"Yes, yes ..."

"Very interesting . . . very pretty . . . very curious . . . yes!"

While still gibbering in this manner and while both of us continued to trail our imaginery fishing nets "in the sea," the great scientist led me in front of a bamboo console on which there were three plaster busts placed in a row, each crowned with an artificial lotus. Pointing at each of them in succession, he named them with such comical gravity that I nearly burst out laughing.

"Master Darwin! Very great naturalist . . . very, very great! Yes!"

I bowed low.

"Master Haeckel . . . very great naturalist . . . not so great as Darwin but still very great ... Master Haeckel here ... like this ... in the sea ... *little fish* ..."

I bowed again. With an even louder voice he placed his crab-red hand on the third bust :

"Master Coqueline . . . very great naturalist . . . very pretty ... very curious!"

"Very interesting!" I agreed.

48

"Yes!"
And with that he dismissed me.

I gave Clara a detailed description of this strange interview and mimed it for her. She laughed like a madwoman.
"Oh, my child, my child, my child . . . how funny you are, my darling little rascal!"
It was the only scientific episode during my mission. It was then I understood what embryology meant!

The following morning, after a savage night of love, we embarked again and sailed towards China.

PART TWO

THE GARDEN OF EVIL

I

"Why haven't you spoken of our dear Annie yet? Haven't you told her of my arrival? Isn't she coming today? Is she still as beautiful as ever?"

"What? You don't know? But Annie is dead, dear heart."

"Dead!" I cried. "It's not possible . . . You're teasing me . . .

I looked at Clara. Divinely calm and pretty and naked under her transparent tunic of yellow silk, she was reclining lazily on a tiger skin. Her head was supported by cushions and with her ring-laden fingers she was toying with a long lock of her loosened hair. A dog from Laos, with red fur was sleeping near her, its snout on her thigh and one paw on her breast.

"What?" repeated Clara, "you didn't know? How funny!"

Smiling and stretching like some sleek animal she explained :

"It was something horrible, darling! Annie died of leprosy . . . that terrifying leprosy they call elephantiasis for everything is terrifying here . . . love, illness, death and flowers! I've never wept so much I assure you . . . I loved her so much and she was so beautiful—so strangely beautiful!"

After a long and graceful sigh she added :

"Never again will we know the bitter taste of her kisses . . . It's a great pity!"

"So it's true then?" I stammered. "But how did it happen?"

"I don't know . . . There are so many mysteries here . . . so many things we can't understand . . . The two of us would often go out on the river in the evenings. I must tell you that at that time there was an Indian dancing-girl from Benares in a flower-boat . . . a maddeningly exciting creature, my darling . . . who had learned certain cursed rites of the old Brahmin cults from the priests . . . It might have been that or something else . . . One night as we were coming back from the river, Annie complained of piercing pains in her head and her kidneys. The next day, her body was covered all over with little purple spots. Her skin which was pinker and even finer to the touch than an althoea flower, hardened, swelled and became ash-grey while great tumours and monstrous swellings rose on its surface. It was something frightful. And then the disease which had at first attacked her legs moved up her thighs, her belly, her breasts and her face . . . Oh her face! her face! Imagine an enormous pouch, a horrible goatskin, grey all over and streaked with brown blood and which wobbled and swung every time she moved . . . And her eyes—her eyes, dear love!—all you could see of them were red, sweating thin buttons . . . I still ask myself if it really could have happened!"

She wound her golden lock of hair around her finger. The sleeping dog's paw moved over the silk and uncovered one of her breasts entirely, with its stiff, pointing nipple as pink as a young flower.

"Yes, I still wonder sometimes whether I'm not dreaming," she said.

"Clara!" I cried, overwhelmed with horror, "say no more to me . . . I want the image of our divine Annie to remain intact in my memory. How can I rid my mind of

51

this nightmare now? Don't tell me any more or else only tell me of Annie when she was so beautiful—too beautiful! . . ."

But Clara was not listening to me. She went on :

"Annie isolated herself . . . she shut herself up in her house, alone with a Chinese governess who tended her. She sent away all her women and no longer wanted to see anyone—not even me . . . She sent for the most skilful English physicians and the most famous Tibetan sorcerers —those who know the magic words and can resurrect the dead but they all declared themselves to be powerless . . . You are never cured from this illness but neither do you die from it . . . It's horrible! Then she killed herself . . . A few drops of poison and that was the end of the most beautiful of women."

Horror nailed my tongue to my palate. I looked at Clara without finding a single word to say.

"I learned a truly curious detail from the Chinese governess," Clara continued, "and one which enchanted me . . . You know how Annie loved pearls . . . She had some which were incomparable . . . the most marvellous in the world, I believe . . . You remember with what a physical kind of joy and with what carnal rapture she would put them on? Well, when she was ill, this passion of hers became a madness . . . a fury . . . like love! All day long, she would touch them, caress and kiss them. She would make cushions, necklaces, mantles and coats with them. But then something extraordinary happened : the pearls died on her skin . . . they first became dull, little by little and then finally lost their lustre altogether and no longer reflected any light in their water. A few days later, infected by the leprosy, they changed into tiny round cinders . . . They were dead, dead like people, my dear love . . . Did you know that pearls have souls? I find the thought exciting and delicious. Since then, I think of it every day . . ."

After a short pause she went on :

"And that's not all! Many times, Annie had expressed the desire to be taken when she was dead to the little Parsee cemetery over there on the hill of the Blue Dog. She wanted her body to be torn to pieces by the beaks of vultures... You know what strange and violent ideas she had in everything! Well, the vultures refused this royal feast that she offered them. They fled from her corpse making frightful cries... It had to be burnt."

"But why didn't you write me all this?" I asked Clara reproachfully.

With slow, charming gestures, Clara smoothed the reddish gold of her hair, caressed the red fur of the dog which had wakened, and negligently said:

"Really? Didn't I write you about any of this? You're sure? I must have forgotten... Poor Annie!"

She added:

"Since this great misfortune everything bores me here... I'm too alone... I would like to die... to die... I too ...Oh, I assure you! And if you hadn't come back I really do believe that I would have died already."

She threw her head back on the cushions, displayed even more of her bare bosom and then smiled, with a strange smile which was that of both a child and a prostitute:

"Do my breasts still please you? Do you still find me beautiful? Well then, why did you go away for so long? Yes, yes, I know... don't tell me... I know... You're a little fool, my dear love!"

I could have wept; I couldn't... I would have liked to have talked to her but even that I couldn't..

We were in the garden, under the golden kiosk with its blue and white clusters of wistaria falling down from above and we had just finished taking tea. Sparkling beetles were buzzing amid the leaves, rose-chafers were vibrating and dying in the swooning hearts of the roses, and through the open door in the north wall of the garden we could see the

53

long stalks of yellow irises streaked with purple flames all around a fountain where storks slept in the soft mauve shadows.

All of a sudden, Clara asked me :

"Would you like us to go and feed the Chinese convicts? It's very curious and very amusing . . . It's really the only elegant and original distraction we have in this lost corner of China . . . Would you like that, my little love?"

I felt tired, my head was heavy and all my being was invaded with the fever of this frightening climate . . . Moreover, the description of Annie's death had brought consternation to my soul. And then, the heat outside was deadly as poison . . .

"I don't know what you're asking me, my dear Clara, but I still haven't recovered from this long journey across the plains and the forests . . . As for the sun—I'm more afraid of it than death! And then, I would so like to devote myself to you entirely and for you to be all mine today . . ."

"So that's it! If we were in Europe and I had asked you to accompany me to the races, to the theatre, you wouldn't have hesitated . . . But this is far more beautiful than the races."

"Be a good girl! Tomorrow, if you like?"

"Oh, tomorrow!" said Clara with an astonished pout and an air of sweet reproach, "Always tomorrow! Don't you know then that it's impossible tomorrow? Tomorrow? But it's quite forbidden . . . The doors of the penal yard are shut . . . even to me . . . You can only feed the convicts on Wednesdays—didn't you know? If we miss this visit today we'll have to wait for a whole long, long week and how boring that would be! A whole week, just think of it! Come, my adorable little weakling . . . Please come with me, I beg you . . . You can at least do that for me."

She half rose from the cushions. Her open tunic revealed corners of her pink, burning flesh between the folds of the cloth, below her waist. With the tips of her fingers she picked a cachet of quinine from a golden tray of sweets on a lacquer tray and after ordering me to come near she gently lifted it to my lips.

"You'll see how exciting it is . . . how terribly exciting! You've no idea, my darling . . . And I'll love you all the better tonight! How madly I'll love you tonight! Swallow it, my dear little heart . . . swallow it . . ."

And as I was still sad and reluctant, in order to overcome my last objections she said, with a dark gleam in her eyes :

"Listen! I've seen thieves hung in England, I've seen bull-fights and anarchists being garrotted in Spain; in Russia I've seen beautiful young girls whipped to death even by soldiers; in Italy I've seen living ghosts and spectres in the midst of famines dig up the corpses of cholera victims and eat them greedily; in India by the banks of a river I've seen thousands of naked beings all writhing and twisting in the terrible throes of the plague; in Berlin, one evening, I saw a woman I had loved the night before—a splendid creature in a pink costume—I saw her devoured by a lion in a cage .. . I've seen all these terrors and all these human tortures with my own eyes . . . It was so beautiful! But I've never seen anything as beautiful—do you understand me?—as these Chinese convicts—they are more beautiful than anything! You've no idea . . . I tell you, you can't imagine . . . Annie and I never missed a Wednesday . . . Please come, I beg you!"

"Since it's so beautiful, my darling Clara, and since it gives you so much pleasure," I replied melancholically, "well then, let's go and feed the convicts."

"Really? You're willing?"

Clara showed her joy by clapping her hands, like some infant whom her governess has allowed to torment a little dog. Then she jumped on to my knees, wheedling and feline as she was, and put her naked arms around my neck

55

... And her hair inundated me, covered my face with its golden flames and intoxicating perfumes ...

"How sweet you are, my dear, dear love ... Kiss me ... kiss my neck ... kiss my hair, my darling little scoundrel!"

Her hair had an animal odour which was so powerful and her caresses were so electric that her mere contact with my skin made me forget fevers, fatigues and pains. All at once I could feel new strength and a new heroic fire circulating gaily in my veins.

"Oh, how we're going to amuse ourselves, darling little soul ... When I go to the convicts it makes me feel giddy and my whole body thrills as though with love ... You see, it seems to me ... it seems to me as though I were sinking down to the depths of my body ... to the depths of the darkness of my body ... Your mouth—give me your mouth! Your mouth ... your mouth ... your mouth!"

And lightly, shamelessly and joyously, she leaped off my knees to go to the women whose duty it was to robe her, followed by the frisking red dog.

I was no longer either very sad or very weary ... Clara's kiss, the taste of which lingered on my lips, like the magical taste of opium, had deadened pain, calmed the pulsations of my fever, and banished the image of dead Annie to the point of invisibility ... And I looked at the garden with a mind at peace ...

At peace?

The garden sloped downwards gently, adorned everywhere with rare flowers and precious plants ... From the pagoda a path through enormous camphor-trees led to a red door, in the shape of a temple, which opened on to the countryside. Between the leafy branches of gigantic trees which hid the landscape from me on the left, I could catch glimpses of the river shining under the sun like polished silver. I tried to take an interest in the many decorations of the garden, in its strange flowers and its monstrous vegetation. A man crossed the path, leading two indolent panthers on a leash . . . Near me, in the middle of the lawn there stood an immense bronze statue representing I know not what obscene and cruel divinity . . . There, birds, cranes with blue plumage, red-throated toucans from tropical America, sacred pheasants, ducks crowned with gold and clothed in dazzling purples like warriors of some past age, and multicoloured longirostrals were searching for shade in the shadow of the rocks . . . But neither the birds nor the animals nor the Gods nor the flowers could hold my attention, nor the bizarre palace to my right, between the cedrelas and the bamboos, with its tiers of light-filled terraces garnished with flowers, its shady balconies and its coloured roofs . . . My thoughts were elsewhere, far away, far far away, beyond the seas and the forests . . . They were within me . . . sunk deep within me . . . to my very depths.

At peace?

Hardly had Clara disappeared behind the foliage of the garden than remorse at my being there seized hold of me. Why had I come back? What folly, what cowardice had I obeyed? As you will remember, she had once said to me on the ship : "When you are too unhappy, you will go away!" I had thought myself to be strong, due to all my infamous past, and all I was in reality was a feeble, anxious child . . . Unhappy? Oh yes! I had been so, to the point of the worst sufferings, the most prodigious self-disgust . . . And I had left! By a truly persecuting irony, I had taken advantage of the passage through Canton of an English mission which was on its way to explore the little-known regions of Annam, in order to flee from Clara. It could have meant forgetfulness, maybe, or perhaps death . . . For two years, two long and cruel years, I had walked and walked . . . And there had been neither forgetfulness nor death . . . Despite fatigue and danger and that cursed fever, there had not been one day or one minute when I had been able to cure myself of the frightful poison deposited in

57

my flesh by this woman to whom I felt I was attached and riveted by the frightening putrescence of her soul and her crimes of love, this woman who was a monster and whom I loved for being a monster! I had thought—or had I really thought it?—that I would be uplifted by her love and here I was, sunk lower than ever, to the very depths of that poisonous abyss from whose depths one never rises once one has breathed its odour of corruption. Many times when I was in my tent in the depth of the forest, haunted by fever after long marches, I had believed I could kill her monstrous and persistent image with opium . . . But opium only conjured her up again more clearly, more vividly, more imperiously than ever . . . Then I wrote her mad, insulting, imprecatory letters in which the most violent execration mingled with the most abject adoration . . . She replied with charming, heedless and plaintive letters which I sometimes found awaiting me in the towns and the posts we were passing through . . . She said she was unhappy at being abandoned by me . . . she wept and beseeched me to come back. She found no other pretexts except this one: "You must understand, my darling, that I have not got the soul of your frightful Europe . . . I bear within me the soul of old China which is far more beautiful . . . Isn't it tragic that you can't accept this?" I also learned from one of her letters that she had left Canton where she could no longer bear to live without me to go with Annie to live in another town further to the south of China "which was marvellous" . . . Oh! How had I been able to resist for so long this evil temptation to abandon my companions and regain this cursed and sublime city, this delicious and torturing hell in which Clara breathed and lived . . . in unknown and atrocious raptures of voluptuousness in which I was now dying to partake . . . And so I had come back to her as the murderer comes back to the scene of his crime . . .

The sound of laughter amid the foliage, little cries . . .

58

the frisking of the dog . . . It was Clara . . . She was dressed half in the Chinese and half in the European style . . . A pale mauve silken blouse embroidered with lightly gilded flowers enveloped her slender form and rounded curves with its many folds . . . She wore a large yellow straw hat under which her face appeared like a pink flower in the clear shadow and her little feet were clad in yellow leather slippers . . .

When she came into the pagoda it was like an explosion of perfumes . . .

"You find me oddly dressed, don't you? Oh, you sad man of Europe who hasn't laughed once since he's been back, aren't I beautiful?"

But as I did not rise from the divan where I was reclining :

"Quick, quick, my darling! We must see everything . . . I'll put on my gloves on the way . . . come along . . . come along! No, no! not you!" she added to the leaping dog as it wagged its tail and leaped around her.

She called a boy and told him to follow us with a basket of meat and a little pitchfork.

"Oh, it's so amusing!" she explained to me, "a love of a little basket made by the very best basket-maker in all China. And the pitchfork—you'll see . . . a love of a little pitchfork with platinum teeth encrusted with gold and a handle of green jade . . . green as the sky in the first light of morning . . . as green as poor Annie's eyes once were! Come along! Don't put on that awful undertaker's face, my darling . . . come quickly . . . quickly!"

And we started to walk in the sun, under that dreadful sun which blackened the grass and withered all the peonies in the garden and which weighed down on my skull like a heavy helmet of lead.

The convicts' prison is on the other side of the river whose sinister and black pestilential waters wind between flat banks outside the town. To go there you must make a long detour to a bridge where the market of Meat-for-the-Convicts is held by a bridge thronged with a concourse of elegant persons.

Clara had refused the palanquin. We went down on foot through the garden situated outside the city limits and went along a path bordered here and there with brown boulders or thick hedges of white roses or trimmed privets to the suburbs where the diminished town almost becomes the countryside and where the houses become hovels, each set away from the others in a small enclosure with a bamboo fence. Next came nothing but flowered orchards, market gardens or wastelands. Men stripped bare to the waist and wearing bell-shaped hats were toiling painfully in the sun, planting lilies—those beautiful tiger-lilies with petals like the claws of a sea-spider whose savory bulbs are used as food by the rich. We passed several wretched sheds in which potters were at their wheels and where rag-pickers would squat among enormous baskets and go through the morning's pickings while hungry crows croaked in the sky above them. Further on, we saw a gentle and meticulous old man sitting under an enormous fig-tree by the edge of a fountain, watching birds. At each moment we passed palanquins taking European sailors, who were already drunk, towards the town. And behind us, burning and ascending the city with its temples and its strange red, green and yellow houses crept up the slopes of the hill and glittered in the light.

Clara walked quickly, without pity for my weariness and without heed of the sun which was burning like a furnace and scorching our skin. She walked freely, lithely, boldly and happily. Sometimes, with a tone of jesting reproach, she said :

"How slow you are, darling . . . God, how slow you are ! Let's hope that the doors of the prison won't be open by the time we get there and that the convicts won't already be gorged with food ... That would be awful! Oh, how I would hate you then!"

Now and again she would give me pastilles of witch-hazel which helped my respiration and with mocking eyes she would say :

"Oh, you little woman ... you little, little woman!"

Then, half laughing, half angry, she would begin to run ... and I had great trouble in following her ... Several times I had to stop and regain my breath ... I felt as though my veins were bursting and my heart exploding in my chest. And Clara would repeat in her prattling tone :

"Little woman ... silly little woman!"

The path led to the quayside along the river. Two large steamers were unloading coal and merchandise from Europe and some junks were getting ready for a fishing expedition; a large number of sampans with their multi-coloured tents were sleeping at anchor, rocked by the slight choppiness of the waves. There was not a breath of breeze.

The quayside disgusted me. It was filthy and full of potholes, covered with black dust and strewn with fish entrails. Stinking odours, the sound of brawls the shrilling of flutes and the barking of dogs could be heard from the depths of the hovels bordering it : verminous tea-houses, cut-throat shops and disreputable looking workshops. Clara laughingly showed me a kind of little stall in which por-tion of rats and quarters of dogs, rotten fish, scrawny chickens rubbed with copal, bunches of bananas and blood-covered bats were displayed for sale in rows, on leaves or else threaded together on the same spit.

As we drew near, the smells became more unbearable, and the filth thicker underfoot. On the river, the boats were huddled and jostling together in a motley collection of sinister bowsprits and torn rags of sail. On the boats lived a dense population of fishermen and pirates—dreadful sea-devils with tanned faces, lips reddened with betel nuts, and eyes that sent a shiver down your spine. They were playing at dice, shouting, fighting; others, more peaceful, were emptying fish which they then dried in garlands in the sun, threading them on cords ... Still others were training monkeys to perform countless pretty little tricks and obscenities.

"Amusing, isn't it?" said Clara "To think that there's thirty thousand of them and that they've got no other home than their boats! The devil knows what they do!"

She lifted her skirts, revealing her trim and lively ankles, and for a long time we followed the horrible path until we came to the bridge with its bizarre superstructure and five massive arches, painted in violent colours, over a river where great pools of oil whirled and sank amid the eddies and currents.

On the bridge the spectacle changed but the smell worsened—that smell so peculiar to China which one finds in the towns, the forests and the plains and which reminds one ceaselessly of corruption and death.

Small boutiques in the shape of pagodas, tents in the shape of kiosks draped with light coloured, silken cloths and enormous parasols planted on top of chariots and carts were all huddled together. In these boutiques and under these tents and parasols, obese merchants with hippopotamus bellies, clothed in yellow, blue or red robes were shouting and striking gongs to attract customers and were displaying every sort of carrion meat: dead rats, drowned dogs, quarters of deer or horses, putrescent chickens, all heaped up, pell-mell, in large bronze basins.

"Here, here! Come over here! Look and choose! You won't find better anywhere else! There's none more rotten!"

And poking about in the basins they would wave their long metal hooks with revolting hunks of bleeding meat like so many flags, and with horrible grimaces made more horrible still by the red gashes on their horrible faces, they would ceaselessly shout above the din and clamour of gongs

62

and their rivals :

"Here, here! Look and choose . . . You won't find better anywhere else . . . there's none more rotten . . ."

As soon as we had set foot on the bridge, Clara said to me :

"You see, we're late. It's all your fault . . . Let's hurry . . .'

A large crowd of Chinese women and, among them a few English and Russian ladies—for there were few men here apart from the vendors—thronged the bridge. With their dresses embroidered with flowers, their multi-coloured umbrellas, their fans waving like birds, their laughter, their cries of joy and jostle, they all shimmered, glittered, sung and fluttered in the sun like a festival of life and love.

"Here! Here! Come over here!"

Overcome by the crush and the jostling, deafened by the yelping of the vendors and the sonorous vibrations of the gongs, I almost had to fight to penetrate into the crowd and protect Clara from the insults and blows of the others. A grotesque struggle, to tell the truth, since I was without strength or power of resistance. I felt myself carried along in this human tumult like a dead tree swept along in the furious waters of a torrent . . . As for Clara, she hurled herself into the mêlée and enjoyed the brutal contact of the crowd—its rape, so to speak—with a passionate pleasure. At one moment she cried triumphantly :

"Look, darling, my dress is all torn . . . It's delightful!"

We had great trouble in making our way as far as the crowded boutiques, besieged as though they were about to be pillaged.

"Look and choose! You won't find any better anywhere else!"

"Here . . . here!"

Clara took the love of a little pitchfork from the hands of the boy who was following us with his love of a little basket, and poked about with it in the basins.

"Take it! Take it, my dear love!"

I thought my heart was going to stop because of the abominable odour of carrion exhaled by the shops, the rummaging in the basins and all the crowd who were rushing upon the carrion meat as though it had been flowers.

"Clara, dear Clara!" I implored her. "Let's go, I beg you!"

"Oh, how pale you are! But why? Isn't it very amusing?"

"Clara, dear Clara! Let's go, I beg you! I can't stand this smell any longer."

"But it's not a bad smell, my love . . . It's only the smell of death, that's all!"

She did not seem to be ill at ease. No grimace of disgust disfigured her white complexion, as fresh as a cherry flower. From the veiled fire in her eyes, from the flaring of her nostrils one would have said she was enjoying the raptures of love . . . She sniffed the smell of rottenness with delight as though it were a perfume.

"Oh what a lovely, lovely piece!"

With graceful gestures she filled the basket with the revolting debris of rotting flesh. And then, painfully, we went on our way through the over-excited crowd and among the abominable smells.

"Quickly, quickly!"

The convict prison is built by the edge of the river. Its quadrangular walls enclose a space of more than a hundred thousand square yards. Not a single window; no other opening than an immense gateway crowned with red dragons and armed with heavy iron bars. The four corners of the sinister wall were topped by watch towers, square towers with sloping roofs which curled up at the ends. Other, smaller towers punctuated the wall at regular intervals. At night, all these towers were lit like light-houses and projected their denunciatory beams around the prison, on the plain and the river. One side of the wall plunged into the black, deep and foetid waters, its solid supports covered with viscous algae. A low door and a draw bridge communicated with a jetty which extended to the middle of the river and where numerous boats and sampans were moored. Two halberdiers, their lances in their hand, kept guard over the door. To the right of the jetty, a small gun-boat, like one of our own armed sloops, was anchored with its three cannons pointing towards the prison. To the left, as far as the eye could see on the river, some twenty-five or thirty rows of boats hid the far bank with a motley collection of multi-coloured hulks, striped masts, rigging and grey sails. From time to time I could see one of those massive paddle-wheel boats powered by poor wretches shut in a treadmill.

Behind the prison, as far as the grey line of the mountains on the horizon, extends a rocky, undulating wasteland with patches of bistre coloured earth and plots the colour of dried blood where nothing grew but thin maple trees, a few bluish nettles and stunted cherry trees which never blossomed. A scene of infinite desolation! Of overwhelming sadness! For eight months of the year, the sky remains blue, a blue streaked with red like the reflections of a perpetual fire, an implacable blue in which no cloud ever dared adventure. The sun bakes the earth, roasts the rocks, vitrifies the pebbles which crack under your feet with the crackling of broken glass and the rustling of flames. No bird ever ventures into this aery furnace. Nothing lives there except invisible organisms and swarms of bacilli which take on the distinct forms of fever, the plague and death every evening while the sad vapours rise from the banks of the weary river together with the chant of sailors. What a contrast with the other river bank where the rich, thick soil is covered with gardens and orchards and nourishes so many huge trees and wonderful flowers!

After crossing the bridge we were lucky enough to find a

65

palanquin which carried us across the burning plain almost to the prison where the gates were still shut. A group of policemen armed with lances with yellow banners and immense shields which almost cover them from sight were containing the crowd which was large and impatient. At every moment, the crowd grew. Tents had been set up where one could drink tea or nibble sweetmeats and rose and acacia petals rolled in thin, sweet-smelling, sugared wafers. In other tents, musicians were playing the flute and poets were reciting verse while the waving *punka* freshened the burning air and brought a breath of freshness to every face. Itinerant vendors were offering images, old legendary accounts of crimes, pictures of tortures and executions, and strangely obscene prints and ivories. Clara bought a few of these last and said to me :

"See that the Chinese, who people accuse of being barbarians, are, in the contrary more civilised than we are; that they are more civilised in the logic of life and the harmony of nature ! They never consider the act of love as a thing of shame which must be hidden ... On the contrary, they glorify it, they sing of all its gestures and all its caresses like the ancients for whom sex, far from being an object of infamy or an image of impurity, was a God ! See how the whole western art has lost from being forbidden such magnificent expressions of love. With us, eroticism is poor, stupid and cold ... It is always shown with all the tortuous aspects of sin while here it keeps all its vital fullness, all the singing poetry and grandiose throbbing of nature ... But you, you're nothing but a lover of Europe ... a poor, timid, shivering little soul which the Catholic religion has so stupidly indoctrinated with the fear of nature and the hatred for love ... It has falsified and perverted your sense of life ..."

"My dear Clara," I protested, "is it natural that you should search for pleasure in this corruption and excite the herd of your desires with these horrible sights of suffering and death? On the contrary, isn't it a perversion of that Nature whose cult you invoke, to excuse, perhaps, the monstrous and criminal side of your sensuality?"

"No!" said Clara sharply, "since Love and Death are the same! As for corruption, it's the eternal resurrection of Life ... Look ..."

Suddenly she interrupted herself and asked me :

"But why are you saying this to me? How funny you are!"

And with a charming pout she added :

"Isn't it a bore that you don't understand anything! How is it you have never felt that all man's cerebral faculties are revealed to him and become sharpened in—I don't say love—but in lust and that it's by lust alone that you attain the total development of your personality? Look— in the act of love have you never thought, for example, of committing a beautiful crime? Of rising above all social prejudices and all laws, above everything? And if you've never thought of it, then why do you make love?"

"I haven't the strength to argue," I stammered, "it seems that I'm walking in a nightmare ... This sun ... this crowd ... these smells ... and your eyes ... oh! your eyes full of tortures and voluptuousness ... and your voice ... your crime ... it all frightens me ... it all maddens me!"

Clara gave a little mocking laugh.

"Poor sweet!" she sighed comically. "You won't say that this evening when you're lying in my arms and when I'm loving you!"

The crowd was becoming increasingly animated. Bonzes squatting under sunshades were spreading their long red robes around themselves like pools of blood and striking gongs frenziedly as they coarsely insulted the passers-by who appeased their maledictions by throwing large coins into metal jars.

Clara led me to a tent embroidered with peach flowers and made me sit beside her on a pile of cushions. Stroking

67

my forehead with her electric touch, with that hand of hers so rich in oblivion and intoxication, she said :

"My God! How slow it all is, my darling! Every week, it's the same thing . . . They never seem to be opening the gates . . . Why don't you speak? Do I frighten you? Are you glad you came? Are you glad I'm caressing you, my adored, sweet little rascal? Oh, your beautiful tired eyes! It's the fever—and it's myself as well, isn't it? Say that it's me! Would you like some tea? Do you want another quinine pastille?"

"I don't want to be here any longer! I want to sleep!"

"Sleep? How strange you are! Oh, you'll soon see how beautiful it is! How terrible it is! And what extraordinary, unknown, marvellous desires it will awake in your flesh! We'll come back by the river, in my sampan and we'll spend the night in a flower-boat . . . Wouldn't you like that?"

She rapped me lightly on the hands with her fan.

"But you're not listening to me? Why aren't you listening to me? You look pale and sad . . . As a matter of fact, you're not listening to me at all . . ."

She snuggled up against me, close to me, lithely and wheedlingly :

"You're not listening to me, you brute," she went on, "and you're not even caressing me! Caress me darling! Feel how cold and hard my breasts are !"

And then, in a lower voice, with her eyes fastened on me and gleaming with a green, voluptuous and cruel light, she went on :

"Listen! It happened eight days ago . . . I saw something extraordinary . . . Oh, my dear love, I saw a man flogged because he had stolen a fish . . . The judge had simply said : 'One must not always say of a man with a fish in his hand that he is a fisherman' and he had condemned the man to die under the iron rods . . . For a fish, my darling! It happened in the garden of tortures . . . Just imagine, the man was kneeling on the ground with his head resting on a kind of headsman's block—a block that was all black with old blood . . . The man's back and thighs were naked . . . his back and thighs were the colour of old gold! I arrived just as a soldier had taken hold of his pig-tail which he wore very long and tied it to a ring set in a stone slab in the ground . . . Near the victim, another soldier was heating a little iron cane in a stove and then . . . Listen carefully! . . . Are you listening? . . . When the rod was red, the soldier whipped the man on the kidneys, with all his strength . . . The rod went whish! through the air and sank deep into the muscles which sizzled and gave out a little cloud of reddish vapour . . . do you understand? Then, the soldier let the rod cool in the man's swelling flesh and when the wound had closed he violently tore it away again . . . with little bleeding bits of flesh . . . and the man uttered frightful shrieks of pain . . . Then the soldier began again . . . he began again fifteen times! And, my dear little heart, it seemed to me each time as though the rod was entering with every blow into my own kidneys . . . It was atrocious and so sweet!"

As I remained silent she went on :

"It was atrocious and so sweet . . . and if only you knew how beautiful he was, that man! . . . how strong he was! . . . With muscles like a statue's . . . Kiss me, my love, kiss me now!"

Clara's pupils had almost disappeared . . . between her half-closed eyelids all I could see were the whites of her eyes . . . She said again :

"He didn't move . . . They were like little waves on his back . . . Oh, your lips! . . ."

After a few seconds of silence she continued :

"Last year, with Annie, I saw something much more astonishing . . . I saw a man who had raped his mother and then disembowelled her with a knife . . . He seems to have been mad, by the way . . . He was sentenced to the torture of the caress . . . Yes, my darling, isn't it wonderful? . . . Strangers are not allowed to watch this torture which is very rare nowadays . . . But we had given money to the guardian who hid us behind a screen . . . Annie and I saw everything . . . The madman—he didn't look mad—was stretched out on a very low table with his limbs and body tied with strong cords . . . his mouth gagged so that he could neither move nor shout . . . A woman—not beautiful, nor young—with a grave face and entirely dressed in black, wearing a large gold ring around her bare arm, came and knelt beside the madman . . . She seized hold of his member and she set to work . . . Oh, darling! . . . darling . . . if only you had seen it! It lasted for four hours . . . four hours, just think of it! . . . Four hours of terrifying, skilful caresses during which the woman's hands never stopped for a minute and during which her face remained cold and sad! . . . The victim expired in a jet of blood which splashed the face of his tormentor . . . I've never seen anything so atrocious and it was so atrocious, my darling, that Annie and I fainted . . . I'm always thinking of it!"

Regretfully, she added :

"The woman had a big ruby on one of her fingers and during the torture it flashed in the sun like a little red, dancing flame . . . Annie bought it from her . . . I don't know what happened to it . . . I would like to have it . . ."

Clara fell silent, her mind doubtless dwelling on the impure and blood-stained images of her abominable memories . . .

A few minutes later, there was a loud whisper among the tents and the crowd. Through my leaden eyelids which had almost closed despite myself, as though to shut out the horror of this recital, I could see dresses and sunshades and fans, faces that were happy and faces that were accursed, all dancing, whirling, rushing . . . It was like a flow of immense flowers, like the wheeling and dipping of fantastic birds . . .

"The gates, dear little heart," cried Clara, "the gates are opening! Come . . . come quickly! And please don't be sad any more, I beg you! Think of all the beautiful things you will see and which I have told you!"

I got to my feet and seizing me by the arm she dragged me I know not where . . .

The doors of the prison opened on to a large dark corridor. At the end of this corridor but from beyond it, we could hear the muffled sound of a bell. When she heard it, Clara clapped her hands.

Oh, dear love! The bell! The bell! We're in luck . . . Don't be sad any more . . . don't be ill, I beg you!"

People were pushing so furiously at the entrance to the prison that the policemen had difficulty in bringing a semblance of order into all this tumult. There were cacklings, cries, chokings, the rustling of dresses and the rattle of sunshades and it was in the midst of this mêlée that Clara threw herself, more resolute, more exalted than ever after hearing this bell while I never once dreamed of asking her why the bell rang thus and what was the meaning of its muffled little tolling—that far away little tolling which gave her so much pleasure! . . .

"The bell . . . the bell! Come!"

But we could not go forward despite the efforts of the boys carrying baskets who tried with their elbows to forge a passage through the crowd for their mistresses. Tall, terribly thin porters with grimacing faces, and bare, seamed chests under their rags were holding up baskets full of meat which the sun was making decompose all the more rapidly and in which millions of tiny larva were swarming. Spectres of crime and famine, images of nightmares, and massacres, demons resurrected from the oldest and most terrifying legends of ancient China—I saw them all around me including one with a sinister, twisting little

71

beard and a saw-like grin that revealed his betel-stained fangs. Others were insulting each other and cruelly pulling each other's pig-tails; still others, with the slinking skill of wild animals, were wending their way through the human jungle, searching pockets, cutting purses and picking jewels and then vanishing with their booty.

"The bell! the bell!" Clara was saying again.

"What bell?"

"You'll see! It's a surprise!"

The odours arising from the crowd—odours of lavatories and the slaughter-house combined, the stink of carrion and the scent of living flesh—disgusted me and froze my marrow. I had the same feeling of lethargic torpor that I had felt so often in the forests of Annam in the evenings when the miasma were rising from the deep ditches and lying in wait with death behind every flower, every leaf, every blade of grass. At the same time, pushed and jostled from every side, and almost out of breath, I almost fainted.

"Clara! Clara!" I called out.

She made me breathe salts whose cordial power somewhat restored me. She herself was free and joyous in the midst of this crowd whose odours she inhaled and whose most repulsive clutches she experienced with a kind of swooning voluptuousness. She offered her body—her whole slim and quivering body—to brutalities, blows and scratchings. Her white skin became a fiery pink; her eyes had the misty brilliance of sexual joy and her lips swelled like hard rosebuds, about to blossom forth . . . She again said to me, with mocking pity :

"Oh, you little woman! little woman! little woman! You'll never be anything else than a silly little woman!"

After the dazzling, blinding light outside, once we had come to the corridor it seemed to be pitch dark. Then, as the darkness gradually lightened, I was able to see where I was.

The corridor was vast and lit from above by a skylight whose thick glass let pass the feeble light of an aquarium. A sensation of damp freshness, almost of cold, enveloped me like the caress of a spring. The walls were sweating like those of subterranean grottoes. Under my feet which had been burned by the pebbles of the plain, the sand strewn on the flagstones in the corridor had the softness of dunes near the sea . . . I took great breaths of air and Clara said :

"You see how kind they are to the convicts here . . . At least, they have fresh air."

"But where are they?" I demanded. "All I can see here are walls!"

Clara smiled.

"How curious you are! Now you're even more impatient than I! Wait . . . wait a little ! Soon, my darling . . . Stop !"

She had come to a halt and she pointed towards a vague point along the corridor, her eyes even brighter, her nostrils quivering, and her ears pricked up like those of a deer in the forest.

"Can you hear? It is they ! Can you hear?"

Then, beyond the cries of the crowd as it invaded the corridor, beyond the buzz of voices I could detect cries and muffled laments, the clanking of chains and the wheezing of breaths like bellows, and the strange, prolonged groans of wild animals. It seemed to come from the depths of the wall or from under the ground . . . from the very abysses of death itself . . . I know not where . . .

"Can you hear?" Clara said again. "It is they . . . you will see them soon . . . let's go on ! Take my arm . . . Look well—there they are !"

We went on again, followed by the boy who was attentively observing his mistress's movements. The frightful odour of corpses accompanied us always, increased by other odours whose ammoniacal harshness stung our eyes and throats.

The bell was still tolling further on . . . further on . . .

slowly and softly and muffled like the groans of a dying man. For the third time, Clara said :

"Oh, that bell! He's dying . . . dying, my darling . . . maybe we'll see him."

All of a sudden, I felt her nervous fingers sinking into my arm.

"My darling . . . my darling! On your right! How horrible!"

I quickly turned my head . . . The infernal procession had started.

To my right I could see vast cells in the wall, or rather, vast cages shut in by bars and separated from each other by thick stone partitions. The first ten were occupied, each by ten prisoners, and all ten cells were the same. Their necks fastened tight in a flat iron collar so large that it was impossible to see their bodies, they looked like terrifying, decapitated heads laid on a table. Squatting in their own filth, with their hands and legs in chains, they could not stand up straight or lie down or ever recline at rest. The slightest movement of the iron collar around their bleeding, raw necks made them shriek with pain and yell atrocious insults intended for us, mingled with supplications to the Gods.

I was dumb with horror.

Lightly, with a pretty shudder and exquisite gestures, Clara plunged her fork into the basket being held by the boy and plucked several small pieces of meat which she graciously threw into the cage between the bars. The ten heads swung in unison on their collars and all at once twenty staring eyes glared redly at the meat with a look of terror and hunger. Then, the same cry of pain came out of ten twisted mouths . . . Conscious of their powerlessness, the prisoners no longer moved. They remained still, their heads slightly inclined as though about to roll down the slope of their great collars, their features pale, convulsed in a rigid grimace or a kind of motionless snarl.

74

"They can't eat," explained Clara. "They can't reach the meat . . . My word! With such shackles as those it's understandable . . . But it's not very new . . . It's simply the torment of Tantalus made ten times worse by the horror of the Chinese imagination . . . Still, would you believe there could ever be such unhappy wretches?"

She threw another small piece of carrion meat which fell on the edge of one of the iron collars and made it oscillate slightly . . . Her gesture was greeted with low gruntings; an even more ferocious and desperate hatred flamed in all twenty eyes at once . . . Instinctively, Clara. stepped back.

"You see," she continued in a less assured tone, "it amuses them when I give them meat . . . it distracts these poor devils for a moment . . . it gives them a bit of illusion . . . Let's go on . . . Let's go on!"

We slowly passed the ten cages. Women who had stopped were either shrieking or bursting into laughter or else making impassioned miming gestures. I saw a very blonde Russian girl with a cold, white look holding a vile piece of green corruption on the end of her umbrella and offering it to the prisoners, withdrawing it and then holding it forward again. Drawing back their lips and revealing fangs like those of wild dogs, with famished expressions that were no longer human, the prisoners tried to snatch the food which always fled from their mouths, sticky with dribble. Some curious women onlookers were following every move in this cruel game with an attentive, amused air.

"What hussies!" said Clara, seriously indignant. "Really, there are women who respect nothing. It's shameful!"

I asked her:

"What crimes did they commit to be tortured in this way?"

She replied absent-mindedly:

"I don't know . . . For nothing perhaps, or for some

small offence, no doubt . . . Probably for some small shop theft . . . Anyway, they are only ordinary people . . . port vagabonds and paupers! They don't interest me very much . . . But there are others—you'll see my poet soon . . . Yes, I've got a favourite here and he happens to be a poet! Isn't it funny? Oh, but he's a great poet, you know! He wrote an admirable satire against a prince who had robbed the treasury and he hates the English . . . They brought him to me one evening, two years ago . . . He sang delightfully . . . But it's in satire that he's truly marvellous . . . You'll see him. He's the handsomest of them all . . . Unless he's dead already! My word, with this diet it wouldn't be surprising . . . What pains me the most is that he no longer recognises me . . . I speak to him . . . I sing his poems to him and he doesn't recognise them . . . It's really horrible isn't it? Oh well, it's amusing enough after all . . ."

She was trying to be gay but her gaiety rang false. Her face was grave, her nostrils were quivering more intensely . . . She leaned on my arm more heavily and I could feel her whole body trembling . . .

I also noticed that on the left hand wall in each cell there was a deep niche. Each niche contained painted sculptures which, with that frightening realism peculiar to Far Eastern art, represented every kind of torture in use in China : the scenes of decapitation, strangulation, flaying alive and cutting to pieces . . . the science of tortures taken to a point of refinement unknown to our western cruelty by a devilish and mathematically-minded cruelty. A museum of frightfulness and despair in which no element of human ferocity had been omitted and whose precise images acted as a reminder for every minute of every day of the ingenious death that their executioners were preparing for their victims . . .

"Don't look at that!" said Clara with a scornful pout. "They are only painted carvings, my love . . . Look over here where it's all real . . . Look! There he is! My poet!"

She abruptly stopped in front of the cage.

A pale, fleshless face scarred with skeleton-like seams with the cheekbones bursting through the gangrene-eaten skin, jaws bared by the trembling withdrawal of the lips, was pressed against the bars between two long, bony clutching hands, as dry and clawlike as a bird's talons! This face from which all trace of humanity had disappeared for ever, and its blood-filled eyes, and these scabby claws of hands terrified me. I instinctively moved backwards to avoid feeling the plague-ridden breath from that mouth on my skin and to escape being wounded by those talons... But Clara quickly brought me back to the cage and made me look again. At the back of the cage, in the terrifying shadows, five living beings which had once been men were walking... walking... turning... and turning ... chests bared and skulls black with the clotted blood of ancient wounds... Panting, barking and shrieking they tried in vain to shatter the solid stone of the wall by hurling themselves against it . . . Then they began to walk and turn again with all the litheness of wild beasts and the obscene movements of monkeys... A large transverse plank hid their lower extremities from sight and from the invisible floor of the cell there arose a suffocating, deadly odour.

"Good-day to you, poet!" said Clara, addressing herself to the Face. "I'm kind, aren't I? I've come to see you again, my poor dear man! Do you recognise me today? No? Why don't you recognise me? I'm still beautiful and I loved you once, one evening!"

The Face did not move. Its eyes never left the basket of meat that the boy was carrying and from its throat there issued forth the harsh bark of an animal.

"Are you hungry?" Clara said. I'll give you something to eat... For you, I've chosen the best bits in the market but first would you like me to recite your poem: *My three mistresses?* Would you like that? It'll give you pleasure

77

to hear it."

And she recited :

I have three mistresses.

The first has a mind as nimble as a bamboo leaf,

Her light and merry humour is like that of the feathery leaf of the elulalia,

Her eye is like the lotus,

Her breasts are as firm as the cedar tree.

Her hair gathered in a single plait falls on her golden shoulders like a black serpent.

Her voice has the softness of mountain honey.

Her hips are slender and graceful.

Her thighs have the roundness of the smooth trunk of the banana tree.

She walks with the gaiety of the young elephant.

She loves pleasure, knows how to give it birth and how to vary it.

I have three mistresses.

Clara stopped.

"Don't you remember?" she asked. "Don't you like my voice anymore?"

The Face did not move. It seemed to have heard nothing. Its eyes were still devouring the horrible basket and its saliva-dripping tongue rattled in its mouth.

"Come now!" said Clara . . . "Listen some more and then you'll eat if you are hungry!"

And in her slow, rhythmic voice she continued :

I have three mistresses.

The second has abundant hair which shines and falls in long silken garlands.

Her look would trouble the God of love.

And bring a blush to the shepherd girls.

The body of this graceful woman-serpent is like a golden liana.

Her ear-rings are heavy with precious stones,
Like a flower heavy with frost on a cold and sunny
    morning.
Her garments are summer gardens
And temples on a feast day.
And her hard, swelling breasts shine like two golden
    vases filled with intoxicating liquors and heady
    perfumes.
I have three mistresses.

The Face barked while the five other prisoners paced
up and down and wheeled in the cage and repeated the
sinister barking sound.
Clara continued :

I have three mistresses.
The hair of the third is plaited and coiled on her head
And never has it known the sweetness of perfumed oils.
Her face full of passion is deformed.
Her body is like that of a pig
Which would always seem to be angry
For always she grunts and she grumbles.
Her breasts and womb exhale the odour of fish.
She is dirty in all her person.
She eats everything and drinks to excess.
Her dull eyes are always rheumy
And her bed is more repulsive than the nest of the crow.
And it is she I love
And it is she I love for there is something more mysteri-
    ously attractive than beauty and that is divine corrup-
    tion.
Corruption in whom the eternal fire of life resides
And which elaborates the eternal renewal of metamor-
    phoses !
I have three mistresses . . .

The poem had ended. Clara fell silent.

Its eyes avidly fixed on the basket, the Face had never stopped barking during the recital of the last verse.

Sadly, Clara said to me:

"You see . . . He doesn't remember anything any more! He has lost the memory of his own verses as he has lost that of my face . . . And that mouth of his that I once kissed no longer knows the language of men! Isn't it incredible?"

She chose the best and biggest piece of meat in the basket and with her bust swelling prettily, she offered it on the end of the fork to the fleshless Face whose eyes were gleaming like two small charcoals.

"Eat, poor poet! Go on, eat!" she said.

With the movements of a famished beast, the poet seized the horrible stinking piece of rotten meat in his claws and carried it to his jaws where, for an instant, I could see it hanging between his dog-like fangs . . . But all of a sudden there were roars and bounds in the excited cage. All I could see were naked torsos mingling, pressed together, clasped by long thin arms and torn by teeth and claws with twisted faces tearing at the meat! And then I could see nothing . . . But I could hear the sound of struggle at the back of the cage and the harsh, wheezing panting of racked chests, the fall of bodies, the trampling of flesh, the cracking of bones, the dull thuds of blows and the groans of dying men! More barks . . . more death rattles . . . and then silence and nothingness!

Clara was pressing her body against mine and trembling all over.

"Oh, my darling! My darling!"

I shouted at her:

"Throw them all the meat. Can't you see that they're killing each other?"

She hugged me and wound herself around me even more tightly.

"Kiss me. Caress me . . . It's horrible . . . it's too horrible !"

And raising her face she gave me a ferocious kiss and said :

"I can't hear anymore . . . They're dead! Do you think they're all dead?"

When we looked at the cage again, a pale, fleshless, blood-covered Face was pressed against the bars and staring at us, almost with pride . . . A scrap of meat was dangling from its lips among threads of purple dribble . . . Its chest was heaving.

Clara clapped her hands but her voice was still trembling :

"It's him! It's my poet! He's the strongest!"

She threw him all the meat in the basket and then, with a choking voice, said :

"I'm stifling somewhat . . . And you too . . . You're pale, my love . . . Let's go and get a breath of fresh air in the Garden of Tortures . . ."

Small drops of perspiration were beading her forehead. She wiped them away and then, turning to the poet, she made a slight gesture with her ungloved hand and said :

"I'm glad you were the strongest today! Eat! Eat! I shall come to see you again . . . Farewell."

She dismissed the boy who was now useless. We went along the corridor quickly despite the press of the crowd, and took care not to look either to the left or the right.

The bell was still tolling but its vibrations diminished until they were no more than a slight breeze . . . a muffled cry of a child behind a thick curtain.

"Why is this bell ringing? Where does it come from?" I asked.

"What? You don't know? But it's the bell of the Garden of Tortures! Just imagine it . . . They tie a victim and put him under the bell and then they ring it at full peal until the vibrations have killed him! And when he's about to die, they ring it softly, softly, so that death won't come too quickly . . . Can you hear?"

I was going to speak but Clara put her open fan across my lips :

"No! Be quiet! Don't say anything! Listen to me, my love! And think of what a terrible death it must be, with those vibrations under the bell . . . Come with me . . . And don't say a word . . . not a word . . ."

When we came out of the corridor, the bell was no louder than the hum of an insect . . . or the barely perceptible flutterings of wings in the distance.

The Garden of Tortures occupies an immense quadrilateral space in the centre of the prison and is enclosed by walls with the stones covered from view by a thick vestment of climbing roses and plants. It was created towards the middle of the last century by Li-Pei-Hang, the superintendent of the Imperial Gardens and the most expert botanist in China. In the collections of the Musée Guimet in Paris one can see many works consecrating his fame and some very curious prints illustrating his most illustrious achievements. The wonderful gardens at Kew—the only gardens of their kind in Europe—are greatly indebted to him from a technical point of view and also as far as their floral ornamentation and landscape architecture is concerned. But they are still far removed from the pure beauty of the Chinese models. As Clara said, they lack that attraction of refinement which comes from mingling tortures with horticulture, and human blood with flowers.

The sandy, stony ground, barren like all the sterile plain around, was ploughed up deeply and covered with fresh earth brought at great expense from the other side of the river. They say that more than thirty thousand coolies perished from the fever during the gigantic work of building terraces that lasted for twenty-two years. But these hetacombs were far from useless. Being mingled with the

earth, like manure—for the dead were buried on the spot—
the slow decompositions of the bodies enriched the soil
so much that no land richer in natural humus can be found
—not even in the heart of the most fantastic tropical forest.
Its extraordinary fecundity is far from exhausted today and
is still maintained thanks to the ordures of prisoners, the
blood of tortured victims and all the organic debris left
every week by the crowd and carefully gathered and skil-
fully mingled with the daily harvest of corpses in special
vats to make a powerful compost which makes the voracious plants even more vigorous and beautiful. Water is in-
geniously diverted from the river and distributed through-
out the garden where, according to the need of each type
of vegetation, it maintains a permanent fresh humidity
besides serving to fill basins and canals in which almost
extinct zoological forms of life are preserved including the
famous six-humped fish celebrated by the poet Yu-Sin and
our own Robert de Montesquiou.

The Chinese are incomparable gardeners, far superior
to our own coarse horticulturalists who think of nothing
but destroying the beauty of plants by disrespectful practices and criminal cross-breeding. The latter are veritable
criminals and I am surprised that no one has decreed the
severest penalties for them in the name of universal life. I
would not even mind if they were guillotined rather than
those poor pale murderers whose social "selectionism" is,
on the contrary, rather praiseworthy and generous-hearted
since most of the time they only destroy ugly old women
and the basest bourgeois who are a perpetual outrage to
life. Not only have they taken infamy to the point of de-
forming the pretty, moving grace of simple flowers, but our
own gardeners have indulged in the degrading jest of
giving the fragility of the rose, the stellar radiance of the
clematis, the heavenly glory of the delphinium, the
heraldic mystery of the iris and the modesty of the violet
the names of old generals and dishonoured politicians. It

is by no means rare in our gardens to find, for example, an iris baptised General Archinard! There are narcissus—narcissus!—with such grotesque names as : The Triumph of President Felix Faure and roses which unprotestingly accept the ridiculous appellation of : President Thiers' Mourning, and violets—timid, frail, exquisite violets!—for which the names of General Skobeleff or Admiral Avellan have not been found insulting! Flowers that are all beauty, light and joy—made to conjure up the whiskers and leathery complexions of old soldiers or the parliamentary vapourings of a minister! Just imagine : flowers proclaiming political opinions or helping to spread electoral propaganda! What aberrations or intellectual crises can be responsible for such blasphemies and outrages against the divinity of living things? If it were possible that some being were soulless enough to conceive a hatred for flowers, he would be found among European—and especially French—gardeners!

Those perfect artists and ingenious poets, the Chinese, have piously preserved their love and fervent worship of flowers as one of the very rare, very ancient traditions which have survived their decadence. And as one must still have names to distinguish one flower from another, they have used graceful analogies, dreamlike images and names of purity or pleasure to perpetuate and harmonise the sensations of sweet charm or violent intoxication that flowers can arouse in us . . . It is thus that the Chinese have honoured peonies, their favourite flower, with the following delightful names, according to each peony's shape and colour, each one being a poem or an entire love story in itself : Young Girl offering her Breasts, or The Water that sleeps beneath the Moon, or Sun in the Forest, or The first Desire of the sleeping Virgin, or My dress is no longer white since when he tore it the Son of Heaven left a little pink on it, or I took pleasure with my friend in the Garden.

84

Clara told me these charming things and then indignantly stamped with her little yellow slippers on the ground and cried out :

"To think they treat them as monkeys or savages, these divine poets who call their flowers *I took my pleasure with my friend in the garden!* ...

The Chinese are right to be proud of the Garden of Tortures which is perhaps the most completely beautiful garden in all of China, where, heaven knows, there are many that are marvellous. There, they have assembled all the rarest essences of their flora, the most delicate and the most robust flowers from the snow-capped slopes of mountains and the fiery furnace of the plains and also those mysterious, fierce plants which hide in the impenetrable depths of forests and which popular superstition endows with the souls of maleficent genii. From the mangrove to the saxatile azalea, from the horny, bifloral violet to the distillatory nepenthes, the twining hibiscus to the stoloniferous helianthus, from the audrosax invisible in its rocky fissure to the most madly interlacing liana, every species was represented by numerous specimens which were gorged with organic nourishment and ritually tended by the cunning gardeners until they achieved a stage of abnormal development and coloration whose prodigious richness we cannot imagine in our own morose climates and soulless gardens.

A vast pond traversed by the arch of a bright green wooden bridge marked the centre of the garden in the hollow of a little valley where a quantity of little sinuous paths and harmoniously undulating, flower-lined paths all met together. Water lilies and nelumbiums brightened the water with their processional leaves and their moving yellow, mauve, white, pink and purple corollae; clusters of irises soared up like lances with strange symbolic birds seemingly perched on their tips; streaked butomus rushes, cyperus plants like flowing hair and giant luzulae mingled their disparate foliages with the phalliform and vulvoid inflorescences of the most fantastic orchids. In a brilliant combination of colours, the gardeners had made artistically trimmed wistaria soar and droop over the water which reflected their clusters of blue berries amid a mass of hart's tongue, globe-flowers and inulae. And cranes with pearl grey plumage, silky tufts and scarlet caruncles, white herons and white storks with the blue throats of Manchuria were walking among the tall grasses in all their indolent grace and sacerdotal majesty.

Here and there, on eminences of earth and red rock tapestried with pygmy heather-plants, tutsan, saxifrage and climbing bushes, slender, graceful pagodas showed the pointed cones of their gold streaked roofs and their delicately curved and boldly sloping eaves above the bamboo plants and cedars. Along every slope every species pullulated : epimedae issuing forth from out of the rocks with their graceful flowers moving and fluttering like insects; orange-tinted day-lilies offering their one-day calyxes to sphinxes; white oenotherae with their blossoms that only lived for one hour; fleshy opuntiae, eomecae, nightshades and carpets, torrents and streams of primulae, those Chinese primulae which are so abundantly polymorphous and of which we have nothing but the most impoverished images in our own hot-houses—all so many charming and bizarre forms and such a melting mass of colours ! . . . And all around the pagodas, between vistas of lawn, and in shimmering perspective the whole garden seemed to be covered with a pink, mauve and white rain, a kind of nuanced swarming, a pearly, fleshy, milky palpitation which was so soft and so changing that no words can ever suffice to express its infinite softness and its inexpressibly fairy-like grace.

How had we been transported there? I had no idea . . .

Under Clara's hand, a door had suddenly opened in the wall of the dark corridor. And all at once, as though a fairy had waved her wand, I had been plunged into a celestial radiance with horizon upon horizon stretching away before me!

I stared, dazzled—dazzled by the softest light, the softest sky, dazzled even by the great blue shadows that the trees softly flung across the grass like so many lazy carpets, dazzled by the moving fairy-like spectacle of the flowers and beds of peonies protected from the deadly glare of the sun by delicate shelters of rushes . . . Not far from us, on one of the lawns, a watering machine was pulverising a jet of water in which we could see every colour of the rainbow and through which the grass and the flowers took on all the translucence of precious stones.

I looked avidly, never wearying of the sight. At the time I did not see any of these details which I later assembled; all I saw was a body of mysteries and beauties whose sudden and consoling appearance I did not try to explain to myself. Nor did I ask myself whether it was reality or a dream that was surrounding me . . . I asked nothing . . . I thought of nothing . . . I said nothing . . . Clara was speaking . . . and speaking . . . No doubt she was telling me still more stories . . . I neither listened nor felt her near me. At that moment, she was so far from me! As far away as her voice . . . and so unknown to me!

Gradually, little by little, I regained possession of myself, of my memories, and of the reality of things and I understood why and how it was that I was there . . .

After coming out of that hell, still pale with the terror of those faces, my nostrils still filled with that smell of decay and death, my ears still ringing with those dries of torment, the sight of this garden was like a sudden calm after having first been like an unconscious exaltation or an unreal ascension of my whole being towards the marvels of a country of my dreams . . . It was with delight that I gulped down great mouthfulls of the fresh air that so many fine and gentle perfumes made fragrant . . . It was the ineffable joy of awakening after the oppressive nightmare . . . I savoured this inexpressible impression of deliverance like someone who has been buried alive in a dreadful ossuary and who has succeeded in raising the slab and coming out again into the sunshine with all his flesh intact, his organs free and his soul reborn again . . .

A bench made of bamboo trunks was near me in the shadow of an enormous ash-tree whose purple foliage shone in the sun and gave the impression of a dome built of rubies . . . I sat there or, rather, I let myself fall on it for the joy of all that splendid life was now nearly making me faint from hitherto ignored pleasure.

On my left I could see the stone guardian of this garden, a Buddha squatting on a rock, his tranquil face of sovereign Compassion bathed with the light of the sun and blue sky. Bouquets of flowers and baskets of fruit covered the base of the statue with so many propitiatory perfumed offerings. A young girl in a yellow robe climbed up to the forehead of the compassionate god and piously crowned it with a wreath of lotus flowers and lady's-slipper . . . Swallows were flying around it, uttering little cries of joy . . . And then it was that I thought—with what religious enthusiasm and with what mystical adoration!—of the sublime life of he who, long before our Christ, had preached purity, renunciation and love to men . . .

But leaning over me like Sin was Clara with her red mouth, as red as the poppy, with eyes as green as the greenish-grey of young almonds, and she soon brought me back to reality as she pointed at the garden with a sweeping gesture :

"Look, my love, see what marvellous artists the Chinese are and how they know how to make Nature the accomplice of their refinements of cruelty ! In our own dreadful Europe which has been so long ignorant of beauty, we torture in secret, in the depths of prisons or in public among vile, drunken crowds . . . Here it is among the flowers, among the prodigious enchantment and prodigious silence of all these flowers that they set up their instruments of torture and death, their stakes, their gibbets and their crosses . . . You will see them soon, all so intimately mingled with the splendours of this floral orgy, the harmonies of this unique and magic Nature that they seem to become a part of it, to become the miraculous flowers born of this sun and this light . . ."

But as I was unable to repress a gesture of impatience Clara chided me :

"Fool! Little fool who can't understand anything!"

Her forehead veiled by a harsh shadow, she continued :

"Look! Have you ever been sad or ill at a feast? Then you must have felt how your sadness must have irritated and exasperated others, like an offence against the joy of others' faces and the beauty of things . . . It's an unbearable impression . . . Think of how it must be for the victim about to die under torture . . . Think how the torture must be multiplied in his flesh and in his soul by all the splendour surrounding him . . . and how his agony must be all the more atrocious . . . all the more desperately atrocious, my dear little heart!"

"I was thinking of love," I replied reproachfully, "and here you are talking to me about tortures again, as always!"

"Of course! Since it's the same thing!"

She remained standing next to me, her hands on my shoulders. The red shadows of the ash tree enveloped her as though with a mantle of fire. She sat on the bench and went on :

"And then there are tortures wherever there are men . . . I can't help it, my child, and I try to make the best of it and rejoice in it since blood is a precious aid to pleasure . . . It's the wine of love . . ."

She drew a few naively indecent figures in the sand with the tip of her parasol and said :

"I'm sure you think the Chinese are more ferocious than we are? But they're not ... they're not! We, the English? The things I could tell you! And as for you French ... This is what I once saw in your Algeria on the edge of the desert : one day some soldiers captured a few Arabs ... a few poor Arabs whose only crime had been to flee from the brutalities of their conquerors ... The colonel ordered them to be put to death at once, without any investigation or trial ... And this is what happened : there were thirty of them. They dug thirty holes in the sand and they buried them up to the neck, naked, with their heads shaven, in the midday sun ... And then, so that they wouldn't die too quickly, they sprinkled them with water from time to time as though they were cabbages ... After half an hour, their eyelids were swollen ... their eyes were coming out of their sockets ... their tumefied tongues were swelling inside their horribly gaping mouths ... and the skin was crackling and sizzling on their skulls ... There was no grace, I assure you, and even no terror in the sight of these thirty dead heads sticking out of the ground like so many shapeless pebbles! As for we English—even worse! Oh, I remember the strange feeling I had when I went to Kandy, the ancient, sad capital of Ceylon, and I climbed up the steps of the temple where the English had stupidly slit the throats, without any tortures, of the little Modeljar princes which legends show us to have been so charming, like those Chinese icons, represented with such marvellous artistry, with such a hieratically calm and pure grace, with their golden nimbus and their long joined hands ... I felt that something had been accomplished there, on those sacred steps, still unwashed and blood-spattered after ninety years of violent possession, that was more horrible than any human massacre : the destruction of a precious, moving, innocent beauty ... In that dying and still mysterious India, traces of that double European barbarism remain at every step you take ... The boulevards of Calcutta, the cool Himalayan villas of Darjeeling, the whores of Benares and the luxurious hotels of merchants in Bombay were all powerless to efface the impression of mourning and death left everywhere by the atrocity of massacres without artistry, by vandalism and brute destruction ... On the contrary, they increased it ... Wherever it shows itself, civilisation always shows its face streaked with sterile blood and ruins for ever dead ... Like Attila the Hun it can say : 'Where my horse has passed, the grass will never grow again'. Look here, around you : There's not one grain of sand that hasn't been bathed with blood and this grain of sand itself—what else is it if not the dust of death? But see how generous this blood is and how it fertilises this dust ! Look ! the grass is thick and the flowers blossom ... and love is everywhere !"

Clara's countenance had become ennobled ... A gentle melancholy softened the dark line of her brow and veiled the green flames in her eyes. She continued :

"Oh how sad and poignant the dead little town of Kandy seemed to me that day ! In the torrid heat, a heavy silence hung over it, with the vultures ... A few Hindus were coming out of a temple where they had been bringing flowers to Buddha ... the profound gentleness of their look, the nobility of their foreheads, the suffering feebleness of their fever-wracked bodies and the biblical slowness of their walk all moved me to the very depths of my being ... They seemed like exiles in their native land, near their god so gentle, chained up and guarded by the sepoys ... And in their black eyes there was nothing earthly ... nothing any more except a dream of bodily liberation and a waiting for a light-filled nirvanas ... I do not know what human self-respect prevented me from going on my knees in front of these suffering, venerable fathers of my own race—my parricidal race...I contented myself with greeting them humbly but they passed without seeing me...without seeing my greeting...without seeing the tears in my eyes and the filial emotion that was making my heart swell...and when they had passed I felt that I hated Europe with a hatred that would never die..."

Suddenly changing the subject, she asked me:

"But I'm boring you, aren't I? I don't know why I'm telling you all this...It's of no consequence...I'm mad!"

"No, no, dear Clara," I replied, kissing her hands, "I love it when you talk to me like this...talk to me like this always!"

She went on:

"After I had visited the poor, bare temple only decorated by a gong at the entrance—the last vestige of former richness—and after having inhaled the odour of the flowers strewn before Buddha, I sadly walked back to the town...It was deserted...A grotesque and sinister evocation of western progress—a clergyman—the only human being, was wandering there, sliding past the walls with a lotus flower in his mouth...Despite the blinding sun, he had kept on his caricatural clergyman's uniform as though in a London fog, with his black, soft hat, his long black coat with its stiff, filthy collar, and his black trousers falling in crapulous creases over his massive clodhopper's shoes...This crabbed preacher's uniform went with a white umbrella, a kind of portable and derisory *punka*—the only concession made by this oaf to local customs and the Indian sun that even the English hadn't been able to turn into a sooty fog so far. And I thought—not without irritation—that you can't take a step between the equator and the pole without meeting that squinting face with its rapacious eyes, those crabbed hands and that vile mouth which breathes the terror of the verses of the Bible mingled with stale gin over the charming divinities and adorable myths of child-religions."

She was becoming animated. Her eyes filled with a burning hatred that I had not seen before. Forgetting the place where we were, her recent criminal enthusiasms and her bloodthirsty exaltations, she said :

"Wherever the spilling of blood is to be legally justified, wherever there are piracies to be consecrated, violations to bless, and hideous commerces to protect, there you may be sure of seeing that British hypocrite pursuing the task of his abominable conquests under the pretext of religious proselytism or scientific study. You can see his cunning and ferocious shadow looming over the desolation of vanquished peoples, side by side with the cut-throat soldier and the ransom-grabbing Shylock. In the virgin forests, the European is rightly feared even more than the tiger. On the thresholds of some humble devastated hut, or between houses set on fire, he will always appear after the massacre as he will on the eves of battles, like the army's scavenger, ready to pillage the dead. But he's also the worthy counterpart of his rival, the Catholic missionary, who also brings civilisation at the end of flaming torches, the points of sabres and the tips of bayonets . . . Alas ! China has been invaded and torn by these two scourges . . . In a few years nothing will remain of this marvellous country where I love to live so much !"

She suddenly started up and uttered a cry :

"And the bell, my love ! We can't hear it any more . . . Oh, my God ! He must have died ! While we were talking here they must have carried him off to the charnel house . . . And we won't see it ! It's your fault as well . . . "

She made me get up from the bench.

"Quick, quick, darling !"

"But there's no hurry, my dear Clara . . . We'll see horrors enough always . . . Speak to me as you were speaking to me a month ago when I loved your voice and your eyes so much !"

She grew impatient :

"Quick ... quick! You don't know what you're saying!"

Her eyes had hardened again. Her voice was jerky, her mouth had become imperiously cruel and sensual ... It seemed to me that even the Buddha's face was twisted in the sneering face of an executioner in an evil sunlight ... And I saw the young girl with the offerings receding into the distance along a path, between the flower-beds ... Her yellow robe was tiny, light and brightly coloured like a daffodil.

The path we were following was bordered with peach- and cherry trees, quince and almond trees, some pygmy-sized and trimmed into the strangest shapes, the others growing freely in clusters and shooting out their long, flower laden branches in all directions. I saw a little apple tree with a bright red trunk, leaves and flowers, shaped like a bulging vase and noticed a marvellous tree which the Chinese call the "pear tree with the leaves of a birch". It had the shape of a perfectly straight pyramid, six yards high, with a wide base and tapering, cone-shaped tip and was so covered with flowers that you could see neither leaves nor branches. Countless petals were falling from it while others blossomed and they whirled around the cone and fell slowly on the paths and lawns like so many snowflakes. Further on, the air was impregnated with the subtle scents of the dogrose and the reseda and then we walked past clumps of bushes decorated with the small-flowered deutzias and large pink corymbs of those beautiful Pekinese ligustrinae with hairy leaves and large feathery panicles of white flowers covered with sulphur-coloured dust.

Each step brought me a new joy or a new surprise which caused me to cry out with admiration. Here there

94

was a vine I had once seen in the mountains of Annam, with its large light-coloured, irregularly notched leaves, as large as the leaves of a castor-oil plant and winding its tentacle-like branches around an immense dead tree as far as the summit and then falling down again in cascades and avalanches and sheltering an entire colony of flora blossoming in the base between the naves, colonnades and niches of its crumbling vine-shoots. There, I saw a stephanander exhibiting its paradoxical foliage, as preciously fashioned as a cloisonné enamel and I marvelled at its range of colouring, its peacock green, its steel-blue, its soft pinks, its barbaric purples, its bright yellows and its brown ochres. Nearby, a group of gigantic viburnums as high as oaks were softly waving vast snowy spheres at the end of every branch.

Here and there, kneeling in the grass or perched on red ladders, gardeners were entwining clematis around thin bamboo trellises or winking ipomea and calystegiae around long slender stakes of black wood . . . And everywhere the tall stalks of lilies were rising above the grass, ready to burst into blossom.

All these trees, bushes, clumps of plants, single growths and clusters seemed at first sight to have grown here and there according to no laws but those of hazard, without cultivation, obeying no other will than that of nature, no other caprice but that of life. Not true. On the contrary, the exact position of each plant had been laboriously studied and chosen either to harmonise form and colour or to make one complement and heighten the other, or to create aery vistas and floral perspectives and multiply every effect by combining every decor. The humblest flower and the most gigantic tree all played their part, by their very siting, in the creation of an inflexible harmony and artistic ensemble whose final effect was all the more moving as it seemed to owe nothing to geometry or decorative intent.

95

Everything also seemed to have been disposed by nature's munificence to ensure the triumph of the peony flower.

Instead of turf, the gently sloping banks had been strewn with sweet-smelling wood-ruff and pink crucianellae with the faded pink of old silks and fields of arborescent peonies like sumptuous carpets. Near us a few isolated peonies were stretching their immense red, black, copper, orange and purple calyxes towards us. Others, of dazzling purity, were displaying every most virginal nuance of pink and white and whether they were clustered in a glittering host or standing in solitary meditation by the edges of the path or the foot of trees, or love-lorn along the clumps of bushes, every peony was like the true fairy or miraculous queen of this miraculous garden.

Wherever I looked I could see a peony. On every stone bridge, covered with saxatile plants, whose audacious arches linked each clump of rocks to the next and provided passage from one kiosk to another, there would pass processions of peonies like a festive crowd. Their brilliant corteges ascended every hillock which in its turn would be surrounded by ascending, intersecting and interlacing alleys and paths bordered by tiny silver-hued spindle-trees and hedges of privets. I admired one hillock covered with low, white walls winding in snail-like curves and covered under a sheltering or matting by the most precious species of peony to which skilful artists had given the multiple forms of the espalier. Every gap in these walls was filled with immemorial. tall-stemmed round clusters of peonies in square boxes and the summit of the hillocks would be crowned with thick tufts or free growing bushes of that sacred plant whose blossoming is so ephemeral in Europe and so regular during every season in China. And to my right or my left, near me or lost in the remote distance, I could still see peonies, always, everywhere ... Always there were peonies, peonies and still more peonies ...

Clara had begun to walk very quickly again, almost insensible to all this beauty. She walked with a hard frown on her forehead and eyes aflame... One would have said that she was walking in the grip of some destructive force... She was speaking but I did not hear her, or if I did, it was only so little! The words of "death, charm, torture, love" which fell from her lips ceaselessly seemed to me to be no more that a far-off echo or a tiny tinkling of a bell, scarcely perceptible far in the distance, melting away in the glory, the triumph and the serenely grandiose voluptuousness of all this dazzling life.

Clara was walking... walking... I walked beside her and everywhere there was some new surprise of peonies, dream-like or demented shrubs, blue spindle-trees, violently spotted holly, curling magnolias, dwarf-like cedars with foliage as dishevelled as untidy hair, aralias and tall gramineous plants, giant eulalias with ribbon-like leaves that fell in undulating waves, like the gold-spotted skins of serpents. I also saw tropical trees and unknown growths with impure orchids dangling and swinging from their branches; the Indian banyan-tree rooting itself into the ground with its multiplying branches; immense musas and, in the shade of their leaves, flowers that looked like insects or birds, such as the faery-like strelitzia with its yellow petals that flutter like wings in perpetual flight.

All of a sudden, Clara stopped as though an invisible hand had suddenly descended upon her brutally.

Anxiously, nervously, her nostrils quivering like a doe which has just scented the male, she sniffed the air around her. A shiver, which I knew already as the herald of one of her spasms, ran through her entire body. Her lips at once became redder and fuller...

"Did you smell it?" she asked me in a sharp, dull tone.

"I can smell the scent of peonies filling the garden," I replied.

She impatiently stamped on the ground.

97

"It's not that! Haven't you smelt it? Try to remember!"

And with her nostrils even more distended, and her eyes glittering even more fiercely, she said:

"It smells as it does when I love you!"

She quickly bent over a plant, a thalicter whose long, slender, branchy, stiff, pale violet stalk was standing at attention by the side of the path. Each axillary branch had issued forth from an ivory-coloured sheath in the shape of a penis and ended in a grape-like cluster of little flowers, huddled closely together and covered with pollen . . .

"It's she! . . . It is she! Oh, my darling! . . ."

A powerful, phosphate-like smell, a smell of human seed arose from the plant . . . Clara plucked the stalk and forced me to breathe in the strange odour and then smeared my face with pollen.

"Oh, my darling . . . my darling! What a beautiful plant! How it excites me! It maddens me! Isn't it strange that there are some plants which smell of love? Why, are you saying? Don't you know? Well, I know . . . Why would there be so many flowers looking like our sexes if it wasn't that nature is always crying out to every living being with all its forms and all its scents 'love each other! Make love! Do as the flowers do! There's nothing but love!' Say it too . . . Say that there's nothing but love! Oh, say it quickly, my darling, adored little scoundrel!"

She continued to inhale the scent of the thalicter and to nibble its berries while her lips became covered with pollen. Suddenly, she declared:

"I want it in the garden . . . I want it in my room . . . in the kiosk . . . in the whole house . . . Smell, little heart, smell! . . . A mere plant—isn't it wonderful? Now let's go on! Quickly! Let's hope we aren't too late for the bell!"

With a pout that was both comical and tragic she added:

"Why did you wait so long, on the bench? With all these flowers here! Don't look at them! Don't look at them any more! You'll see them better afterwards . . . after having seen suffering and after seeing death . . . You'll see then how much more beautiful they will be and what ardent passion there is in their perfume! Smell it again, my darling and come with me . . . Feel my breasts . . . How hard they are! The silk of my dress is exciting them . . . You'd say they were being burnt by a hot iron . . . It's delicious . . . come with me . . . "

Clara would not stop before another statue of Buddha with its drawn, time-ravaged face twisting in the sunlight. A woman was offering it flowers of cydonia and each one seemed to me to be a child's tiny heart . . . Going around a corner we passed a litter carried by two men. On it there was moving a kind of parcel of bleeding flesh, a kind of human being whose skin was flayed away in ribbons and trailing like rags along the ground. Although it was impossible to recognise the slightest vestige of humanity in this hideous gaping wound which had once been a man, you could still feel that by some miracle it was breathing. Red drops and trails of blood fell behind it, along the path.

Clara picked two peonies and silently placed them on the litter with a trembling hand. The bearers smiled brutishly, revealing their black gums and lacquered teeth and when they had gone Clara said:

"Oh! I can see the bell . . . I can see the bell . . . "

And all around us and all around the litter as it moved away into the distance, there was a kind of pink, mauve and white rain, a delicately hued swarming, a fleshy, milky palpitation that was so soft and so changing that no words can ever describe the infinite sweetness and the inexpressibly Eden-like charm of the scene . . .

We left the circular path which branched out into other paths which snaked their way to the centre of the garden

99

and which passed alongside a hillock planted with a mass
of rare and precious shrubs, and took a little path which
took us across a hollow directly towards the bell. Both
foot-tracks and paths were strewn with pulverised brick
sand which gave the green of the lawns and the foliage an
extraordinary intensity and a kind of emerald transpar-
ency, as though seen in the light of a chandelier. To our
right there were flower-covered lawns; to our left, still
more shrubs. We saw pink maples, streaked with pale silver,
bright gold, bronze or red copper; mahonias with leaves
the colour of russet leather and as wide as coconut palm-
leaves; eleagnus which seemed to have been covered with
multi-coloured lacquers, pyrites and mica dust; laurels
shimmering with the thousand facets of iridescent crystal;
caladiums with veins the colour of old gold surrounding
embroidered silks and pink lace; blue, mauve and silvery
arbor vitae spotted with sickly yellows and venomous
oranges; yellow tamarisks, green tamarisks, red tamarisks
with branches waving and undulating in the air like so
many small sea-weeds in the ocean; cotton-bushes with
their tufts ceaselessly flying off and floating through the
air; willows amid the joyous swarming of their winged
seeds; clerodendrons with their large incarnadine umbel-
lates opened wide as parasols ... And in the sunlit patches
between all these shrubs there were anemones, buttercups
and heuchera mingling in the grass while in the shady
parts there blossomed strange cryptogams of mosses
covered with tiny white flowers and lichens that looked
like agglomerations of polyps or masses of madrepores. It
was a scene of perpetual enchantment.

And in the midst of this floral enchantment there stood
scaffolds, crucifixes, violent-hued gibbets and black gallows
with frightful demons' masks sneering from their summits;
other gallows for simple strangulation, lower gibbets with
machinery for the dismemberment of bodies. By a diabolical refinement, the tops of these columns of torture were

wreathed with pubescent calystegia, ipomea, lophospermae
and colocynths amid clusters of clematis and atragenae
... Birds sat there, composing their love songs ...

At the foot of one of these gibbets which was as flower-
strewn as a pillar in a garden, a torturer was sitting, his
case of instruments between his legs, wiping his delicate
steel instruments with silken rags. His robe was covered
with patches of blood and his hands looked as if they were
covered by red gloves. All around him, as though around
a carcass, swarms of flies were circling and buzzing ... But
in the midst of all these flowers and perfumes the sight
was neither repellent nor terrible. One would have said
that his robe was covered with a shower of petals fallen
from some nearby quince-tree ... Moreover, he had a
peaceful and jovial pot-belly ... His face, in repose, expressed bonhomie and even cheerfulness—the jovial expression of a surgeon who has just succeeded in accomplishing
a difficult operation. As we passed close by him he looked
up at us and greeted us politely.

Clara spoke to him in English.

"It's a real pity that you didn't come here an hour
earlier," said this good fellow. "You would have seen
something very beautiful—and also something you don't
see every day ... An extraordinary piece of work, milady!
I've reshaped a man from head to foot after having taken
all his skin off! He was so badly built! Ha! ha! ha!"

His belly shook as he laughed, swelling and contracting
with the dull sound of rumbling intestines. A nervous tic
made him draw back the corners of his mouth to his ears
while his eyelids fluttered down and nearly met the ends
of his lips among the greasy folds of his skin in a grimace—or rather, a multitude of grimaces—which gave his
face an expression of cruelty that was both comical and
macabre. Clara asked him :

"It was he no doubt that we met on the litter just
now?"

"Oh! so you met him?" the good man was flattered. "Well, how did you find him?"

"It was horrible!" said Clara in a voice which belied the disgust contained in her exclamation.

Then the torturer explained to us:

"He was a miserable harbour coolie ... no one at all, milady ... He certainly didn't deserve the honour of such a fine piece of work ... It seems he had stolen a bag of rice from the English—our good and dear friends, the English ... When I had taken off his skin and it was only hanging from his shoulders by two little strips, I made him work! Ha! ha! ha! A good idea, really! You would have split your sides laughing ... You would have said he was wearing a—what do you call it? A macfarlane cape? Never had the dog been better dressed, or by a better tailor! But his bones were so hard that I blunted my saw—this lovely saw of mine ..."

A whitish, greasy little morsel had remained between the teeth of the saw. He flicked it with his nail and sent it flying into the grass, among the flowers.

"It's marrow, milady!" he said merrily. "It's cheap enough ..."

Nodding his head he repeated:

"It's cheap enough stuff! We nearly always work on the lower classes ..."

With an air of quiet satisfaction he added:

"Yesterday—my word! It was really curious ... I made a man into a woman ... Heh! heh! heh! You would have been taken in ... I was taken in myself when I looked ... Tomorrow, if the gods are good enough to grant me the favour of having a woman here at this gibbet, I'll make her into a man ... It's less easy! Ha! ha!"

This new outburst of laughter made his triple chin, the folds of his neck and his belly quiver like jelly. A single red, arched line ran from the left corner of his mouth to the corner of his narrow eyelids in the midst of wrinkles and furrows dripping with thin threads of sweat and tears of laughter.

He put his polished and shining saw back in his case which he shut again. The bow was a charming one and beautifully lacquered with a flight of wild geese above a silvery pond with lotuses and irises bathed in the moonlight represented on the lid.

At that moment, the shadow of the gibbet threw an oblique, bar of darkness across his body.

"You see, milady," continued the gossipy old fellow, "just like our beautiful pottery, our beautiful embroidered silks and our beautiful lacquers, our trade is ever more a dying art... Today we no longer know what torture really is... Even though I do me best to preserve the true traditions it's too much for me and I can't stop the decadence all on my own. What do you expect? They recruit torturers anyway, anywhere now! No more examinations, no more competitions and mere favouritism and patronage to decide the choices! And what choices! If only you knew! It's scandalous! In the old days these important functions were only entrusted to genuine scientists and people of worth who knew the anatomy of the human body to perfection, who had diplomas and experience or else a natural gift! Today—get away with you! The least cobbler can claim to fill these honourable and difficult posts.... No more hierarchy or traditions! It's all going... We're living in a time of disorganisation... There's something rotten in China, milady..."

He heaved a great sigh and showed us his red hands and then the case which was shining in the grass beside him.

"And yet, I'm doing my best as you can see, to lift up our abolished prestige... I'm an old conservative, myself, and an intransigent nationalist, and I hate all these new ways being brought us in the name of civilisation by the Europeans and, in particular, the English... I'm not say-

103

ing anything against the English, milady. They are fine people and highly respectable ... But, you must admit that their influence on our ways has been disastrous. Each day they take away something of China's exceptional character. To talk of torture alone, they have done us a great deal of harm ... a great deal of harm ... It's a great pity!"

"But they're still good at it!", interrupted Clara, whose national self-respect had been wounded by this remark for although she was ready to be severe with her compatriots whom she detested, she wanted them to be respected by others.

The torturer shrugged his shoulders and under the impulsion of his nervous tic succeeded in composing his face into the most imperiously comical expression ever seen on a human visage. While we were trying to contain our mirth with the greatest difficulty, despite our horror, he sharply declared:

"No, milady, they don't know anything at all about it. In this respect they are great savages. Look at India—to talk of India only—and see how crude and inartistic they have been! And how stupidly—yes, stupidly—they have wasted death!"

He clasped his bloody hands as though to pray, looked up at the sky and in a voice that seemed to be sobbing with regret he said:

"When you think, milady, of all the admirable things they could have done there and which they have not done—and never will do! ... It's unforgivable!"

"Really!" protested Clara, "you don't know what you're saying!"

"May the evil genii fly away with me if I'm lying!" exclaimed the fat fellow. And then, in a calmer tone and with didactic gestures, he explained:

"In torture as in all things, the English are not artists ... They have all the qualities you may care to mention, milady, but not that one. No, no, no."

"For heavens' sake! They've made all of mankind weep!"

"Bad, milady, very bad" said the torturer, correcting her. "Art does not lie in killing a lot, in cutting throats or exterminating and massacring men in masses ... Really, that's too easy ... Art, milady, lies in knowing how to kill according to rites of beauty of which only we Chinese know the divine secret ... Knowing how to kill! ... Nothing is rarer and yet all is in those four words ... Knowing how to kill! That's to say working on human flesh as a sculptor works on his clay or his piece of ivory ... extracting the whole sum, all the marvels of suffering that it conceals in the depths of its darkness and its mysteries! That's it! You need science, variety, elegance, inventiveness— genius in a word ... But everything's dying out these days ... This Western snobbery which is invading us, all these gunboats, quick-firing cannons, long range rifles, electricity, explosives and I don't know what else, all that makes death collective, administrative and bureaucratic ... all the filth of your progress, in a word ... they are all gradually destroying our beautiful past traditions ... It's only here, in this garden, where they are still being preserved, for better or worse ... where we are at least trying to preserve them for better or worse ... But what difficulties! What obstacles! How many continuous struggles we have! If only you knew! Alas, I feel it can't last much longer ... We are being beaten by mediocrity ... And it's the bourgeois spirit which is triumphing everywhere ... "

His physiognomy then assumed a singular expression of melancholy and pride combined, and his gestures betrayed a profound weariness.

"And yet," he said, "I who am talking to you, milady, I am certainly not anybody ... I can boast of having worked all my life long with selflessness for the glory of our great Empire ... I have always been by far the best in

torture competitions ... Believe me, I have invented truly
sublime and admirable torture which in another age and
under another dynasty would have earned me fortune and
immortality ... Now, I'm scarcely noticed ... I'm not
understood ... Let's be frank : I'm despised ... What do
you want! Today, genius counts for nothing ... no one
accords it the slightest merit ... It's discouraging, I assure
you! Poor China, once so artistic, once so greatly illustrious! Oh, I'm afraid it's ripe for conquest !"

With a gesture of pessimism and exasperation, he
appealed to Clara to confirm this decadence and as for his
grimaces—they were quite indescribable.

"Anyway, milady, isn't it enough to make you weep? It
was I who invented the torture of the rat—may the evil
genii gnaw my liver and twist my testicles if it isn't I ! Oh,
milady, it's an extraordinary torture, I assure you ...
Originality, picturesqueness, psychology, the science of
pain, it has them all ... And to crown it all, it was infinitely comical. It was inspired by that old Chinese gaiety of
ours which is so much forgotten nowadays. Oh, how it
would have appealed to peoples' sense of humour ! What a
resource it would have been when conversation lan-
guishes ! Well, they gave it up. To put it better : they
didn't want it ... And yet, the three trials we conducted
before the judges were a huge success."

"What is this torture of the rat?" asked Clara. "How is
it that I don't know of of it?"

"A masterpiece, milady ... a pure masterpiece !" the fat
fellow affirmed in a thunderous tone as he let his flaccid
body sink back even further into the grass.

"Very well then ... But what is it?"

"A masterpiece! And there you are ... You see ... You
don't know it ... No one knows it ... What a pity ! How
do you expect me not to feel humiliated?"

"Can you describe it to us?"

"Can I describe it? But perfectly ... I shall explain it to

you and you shall judge. Listen carefully ...."

And with precise gestures, the fat fellow described it to us :

Charming milady, you take a condemned man or anyone else—since it isn't necessary for my torture to have a man condemned to anything in particular—who is as young and strong as possible and whose muscles are resistant by virtue of the principle that the more strength there is, the more struggle there is, and the more struggle the more pain! Good ... You undress him ... Good ... And when he is naked you make him kneel, with his back bent, on the ground where you fasten him with chains riveted to iron collars around his neck, his wrists, his hams and his ankles ... Good! I hope I am making myself clear? You then take a large pot with a little hole pierced in the bottom—a flower pot, milady!—and put in it a very large rat which you should have deprived of food for two days previously in order to excite its ferocity. With the pot now inhabited by the rat, you apply it hermetically, like an enormous leech, to the buttocks of the condemned man, fastened to him with a leather strap around his ... Ah, you see what I am coming to? ... "

He maliciously looked at us from out of the corners of his half-shut eyelids, to judge the effect that his words were having on us.

"And then?" asked Clara.

"And then, milady, what do you think you put through the little hole at the bottom of the pot?"

"How should I know?"

The man rubbed his hands, gave a frightful smile, and continued :

"You introduce into the pot an iron rod which you have first heated until it glows red in a little portable stove next to you ... And when you have introduced the iron rod— what happens then? Ah! Ah! Just imagine what happens next, milady!"

"Go on, you old chatterbox!" ordered Clara whose little feet were angrily stamping on the sand of the pathway.

"There, there!" said the torturer soothingly. "A little patience, milady ... And let's proceed with method, if you please ... As I was saying, you put an iron rod made red hot in the fire of a stove through the hole in the bottom of the pot ... The rat wants to flee from the burning touch of the rod and its blinding light ... He panics, jumps, writhes and wriggles, turning around, climbing up the sides of the pot, and running over the buttocks of the man whom he first tickles and then tears with his claws and bites with his sharp teeth as he seeks for an issue through the torn and bleeding flesh ... But there is no issue—none, at least, in the first moments of the rat's panic. And the red hot rod which must be handled with skill and slowness always comes closer to the rat, threatening it and singeing its fur ... What do you think of this prelude?"

He drew breath for a few seconds and then, ponderously and authoritatively declared:

"The great merit in this is that one must be able to prolong this initial operation for as long as possible for the laws of psychology teach us that there is nothing more horrible than the combination on human flesh of tickling and biting ... It can even happen that it makes the victim go mad ... He screams and struggles. His body, which has been left free between the iron collars, palpitates, rises, twists and is shaken by painful shudders ... But his limbs are solidly held by chains and the pot is fastened to him by thongs ... All the victim's movements are designed to excite the rat's fury which is soon increased even more by the intoxication of blood ... It's sublime, milady!"

"And then?" asked Clara, who had paled slightly, in a sharp, shaky tone.

"And then—since I see that you are in a hurry to know the end of this admirable and jovial story and then ... Menaced by the red-hot rod and thanks to the excitement of a few convenient burns, the rat ends by finding an issue—a natural but how ignoble an issue, milady!"

"How horrible!" cried Clara.

"Ah, you see! You don't have to say it! I'm proud of the interest you are taking in my torture...But wait... The rat penetrates into the man's body, by the way you know, and enlarges it with his feet and teeth... Frantically he digs himself a burrow as though in the earth and he dies suffocated in it at the same time as the victim who, after a half hour of inexpressible, incomparable tortures, also ends by succumbing to a haemorrhage if not an excess of suffering or even a stroke brought on by unbearable fright. In any case, no matter what the final cause of death may be, believe me when I say that it is extremely beautiful to see!"

With an air of satisfied pride, he concluded:

"Beautiful, isn't it, milady? Isn't it a wonderful invention—an admirable and even a rather classical masterpiece for which you would hardly hope to find an equivalent in the past? I wouldn't like to be vain, milady, but you must agree that even the demons that used to haunt the forests of Yunnan never dreamed of such a marvel...But the judges wouldn't hear of it! As you can see, I was showing them something infinitely glorious—something that was unique of its kind and which was capable of setting fire to the imagination of our greatest artists and they would not hear of it! They would not hear of anything any more! The return to the classical tradition frightened them...Not to speak of all kinds of moral inhibitions, all painful to relate: intrigue, rivalry, venality, a scorn for justice and a hatred for beauty and heaven knows what else!...I'm sure you would think that they would at least have made me a mandarin after having rendered such a service! Not at all, milady! I was given nothing at all! A characteristic sign of our decadence... Oh, we're a finished people—a dead people! Let the

Japanese come—we're no longer able to resist them..
Goodbye China!"

He fell silent.

The sun was moving towards the west and the shadow of
the gibbet was lengthening on the grass, moving with the
sun. The lawns were becoming a brighter green; a kind of
pink and gold haze rose from the watered flower beds and
each flower was becoming more radiant, more luminous,
and more like some little many-coloured star lost among
the firmament of greenness...A yellow bird with a long
thread of cotton hanging from its beak, was repairing its
nest, hidden in the depths of the foliages decorating the
summit of the torture column at the foot of which the
torturer was sitting.

He began to daydream, with a more placid face, free
from grimaces, and in which cruelty had given way to
melancholy.

"It's just like the flowers!" he murmured after a long
silence.

A black cat came out of the bushes with back arched
and tail waving. It rubbed itself purringly against him and
he stroked it softly. The torturer continued :

"It's just like the flowers! We have also lost the sense of
flowers, for all is related...We no longer know what
flowers are...Would you believe me when I tell you that
they are now sending us flowers from Europe—we who
have the most extraordinary and varied flowers on earth!
What aren't they sending us today? Hats, bicycles, furni-
ture, coffee-grinders, wine and flowers! And if only you
knew the sad stupidities, the sentimental nonsense and the
decadent follies that our poets now pour out over flowers!
It's frightening! Some people even pretend that they're
perverse! Flowers—perverse? Have you ever heard such
nonsense, milady? Flowers are violent, cruel, terrible and
splendid—like love itself!"

He picked a buttercup near him, which was softly waving its petals above the grass of the lawn, and with infinite, slow grace, he lovingly turned it in his fat fingers where the blood had dried in hard shiny patches.

"Isn't it adorable?" he exclaimed, contemplating the flower. "How small and fragile it is and yet it holds all of nature—all the beauty and strength of nature ... It contains the whole world ... A frail and pitiless organism that goes to the very ends of its desire! ... Oh, flowers are far from sentimental, milady ... They make love—nothing but love ... And they make nothing but love, all the time and in every way ... It's all they think of ... Perverse are they? Because they obey the sole law of Life, because they satisfy Life's sole desire which is love? But look at it! Flowers are all sex, milady ... Is there anything more healthy, stronger and more beautiful than sex? Look at these marvellous petals, these silks and velvets, these soft, warm and caressing draperies ... the curtains of the bed-chamber—the draperies of the nuptial chamber and the perfumed bed in which the sexes come together and where they spend their ephemeral and immortal lives swooning with love ... What a wonderful example for us!"

He pulled aside the petals, counted the pollen-laden stamen and with eyes flooded with the tears of his burlesque grief he added:

"Look, milady! One, two, five, ten, twenty ... How they tremble! Look! Sometimes ten males are needed for one female's orgasm! Heh! heh! heh! Sometimes the contrary happens!"

One by one he tore away the petals.

"And when they're gorged with love, then the curtains of the bed are torn and the draperies of the bedroom dissolve and fall away ... And the flowers die for they know there is nothing left for them to do ... They die to be born again later to make love once more!"

He threw the buttercup far away from him and exclaimed:

"Make love, milady . . . make love like the flowers !"

He abruptly picked up his case and stood up, his pigtail crooked, and after saluting us walked away over the lawns, his heavy, swinging body crushing the grass with its myriad flowers. Clara watched him for a few moments and then we continued our walk towards the bell.

"How funny he is!" she said. "He looks like such a merry fellow !"

I stupidly objected :

"How can you say such a thing, my darling Clara? But he's a monster! It's terrifying to think that such a monster can live among mankind! I feel that from now on I'll never escape from the nightmare of his horrible face and his terrifying words . . . "

Clara was sharp in her reply :

"You're upsetting me too! Why do you think the old fellow's a monster? You don't know a thing about him! He's in love with his art—that's all! Just like a sculpture in love with sculpture or a musician in love with music . . . And how wonderfully he speaks of it! How curious and irritating it is that you won't realise that we are in China and not—thank God!—in Hyde Park or the Bois de Boulogne, in the middle of all those horrible bourgeois you love so much! You seem to want customs to be the same everywhere! And what customs! A fine ideal! You don't seem to realise that it would mean dying of boredom and never knowing what it is to travel, my darling !"

Even more reproachfully, she went on :

"You're really not kind to me . . . Not for a minute does your selfishness leave you—not even when I ask you one little favour . . . It's impossible to amuse oneself with you . . . You're never pleased with anything . . . You contradict me in everything I like . . . Not to mention the fact that you have probably made us miss the most beautiful thing of all today !"

She sighed sadly.

"A day lost! I'm out of luck!"

I tried to defend myself and calm her.

"No, no," Clara insisted, "it's too bad. You're not a man. Even when Annie was with us it was the same thing ... You spoilt our pleasure with the way you fainted like a little old lady or a pregnant woman. A person like you should stay at home. Isn't it too awful! We go off, gaily and happily, to amuse ourselves, to see something sublime, and to enjoy the most extraordinary sensations and then we suddenly become sad and it's all finished! No! No! It's really too silly for words!"

She hung even more heavily on my arm and pouted so daintily—a pout half of anger and half of tenderness— that a thrill of desire shot through my veins.

"And to think I do everything you want like a dog!"

Then :

"I'm sure you think me bad because I enjoy things that make you pale and tremble! You think I'm evil and heartless, don't you?"

Without letting me reply, she went on :

"But I become pale too, and I tremble ... If I didn't, I wouldn't enjoy myself. So you think I'm bad?"

"My dear Clara, you're not an evil woman ... You're—"

She interrupted me at once and offered her lips to me :

"I'm not evil ... I don't want you to think that I'm a bad woman ... I'm just a kind-hearted, curious little woman—like all women ... You're just an old fuddy-duddy! I don't love you any more ... There, there ... kiss me hard ... harder ... You're just a silly little love."

Gay and sombre at the same time, with her brow overcast by that shadow it had both in anger and in rapture, she added :

"To think that I'm just a woman—a poor little woman as frail and delicate as a flower and that I'm still the man of the pair of us ... To think that I'm worth ten men like you!"

The desire that her body was arousing in me became mingled with an immense pity for her mad and wayward soul.

"Men!" she said with a slight hiss of scorn, "they don't know what love is nor death which is much more beautiful than love ... They don't know anything and they are always sad! Always crying for no reason and fainting for a mere nothing!"

Changing the subject like a beetle hopping from one flower to the next, she asked :

"Was it true what the old fellow was saying just now?"

"What? What does it matter to you anyway?"

"He was saying that twenty males were sometimes needed for one female flower to have an orgasm! Is it true?"

"But of course it is!"

"He wasn't making fun of us? You're quite sure?"

"How funny you are! Why do you ask me? Why are you looking at me so strangely? It's true!"

"Ah! ..."

She remained lost in thought. Her eyes shut for a few seconds. She began to pant and her bosom heaved. She inclined her head against my chest and softly said :

"I'd like to be a flower ... I'd like ... I'd like everything!"

"Clara!" I beseeched her. "My little Clara!"

I held her tightly in my arms.

"Not you!" she added. "Not you! You'd like to stay a little wet rag of a man all your life!"

After a short pause in which we listened to the crunching of the sand on the path under our footsteps which became ever more heavy, she began to speak again in a sing-song tone :

"And when I'm dead I would like the strongest perfumes to be put in my coffin ... thalicter flowers ... And pictures of sin ... beautiful, burning, naked pictures of sin like those on the walls of my room ... Or else I'd like to be buried without robes and without a shroud in the crypt of the temple of Elephanta among all those strange stone Bacchantes who caress and tear themselves with all the fury of lust ... Oh, my darling, I'd like to be already dead!"

Abruptly, she enquired :

"When you're dead—do the feet touch the end of the coffin?"

"Clara!" I implored her, "why are you always talking of death? How do you expect me not to be sad? I beg you, don't make me go quite crazy ... Forget these dreadful ideas which torment me and let's go back ... For pity's sake, Clara, let's go back!"

She didn't listen to me and went on in a singing tone which might have been one of irony or one of emotion—I didn't know :

"If you're with me when I die, my darling little heart, listen to me carefully! You must put a pretty cushion of yellow silk between my poor little feet and the wood of the coffin ... And then, you must kill my lovely Laotian dog and lay it all bleeding against me—as it lies against me now, with one paw on my thigh and another on my breast ... And then ... and then ... You must kiss me for a long time, my darling love, on my teeth and on my hair ... And you'll say things to me ... such pretty things ... things which soothe and burn ... as you're making love to me ... Won't you, my darling? Promise me! There now, don't put on that undertaker's face! It's not dying that is sad—it's living when one isn't happy. Swear it! Swear that you'll promise me!"

"Clara, I beg you! Be quiet!"

No doubt I was at the end of my tether ... My eyes flooded with tears. I couldn't say why these tears were welling up in me but far from causing me distress they brought me relief. Clara was mistaken in seeing herself as

115

the cause. It was not for her that I was crying, nor for her sin, nor out of pity for her poor sick soul, nor for the picture of her death that she had been conjuring up ... It was, perhaps, for myself alone that I was crying. I was crying because of my presence in that garden, because of that accursed love of mine in which I felt there were generous impulses, lofty desires and noble ambitions which were being profaned by the impure touch of those kisses of which I was both so ashamed and so desirous? Well, it was for none of those reasons! Why should I lie to myself? They were purely physical tears ... tears of weakness, of weariness and fever ... They were tears of exhaustion brought on by sights too harsh for one of my depressed sensibilities, by odours too strong for my sense of smell, by the continuous vacillation between impotence and exasperation of my carnal desires ... They were women's tears! Tears that meant nothing!

Sure of herself, sure of herself lying dead in her coffin and being wept over by me, and happy of her power over me, Clara became deliciously wheedling.

"Poor sweet!" she sighed. "You're crying! Well then, say at once that the fat old fellow was a kind man ... Say it to please me and I'll be quiet and never talk of death again ... never ... Come! Say it at once!"

Out of cowardice and also to finish once and for all with all these macabre ideas of hers, I did what she wanted. With a loud outburst of joy she flung her arms around my neck, kissed me on the lips, and dried my eyes, crying:

"Oh, how sweet you are! My sweet little baby! My darling little baby! I'm just a nasty woman ... a nasty little woman who teases you the whole time and makes you cry. And then ... The old fat fellow is a monster ... I hate him ... I don't want you to kill my lovely dog from Laos and I don't want to die ... I adore you ... And then ... and then ... it was only for a joke, you

116

understand? Don't cry any more! Smile now...smile with your eyes which are so kind and that mouth of yours which says such sweet things...Your mouth! Your mouth! Let's hurry! I love walking quickly on your arm!"

Her parasol floated as lightly, as brightly and as gaily as a large butterfly over our two heads as we walked cheek to cheek.

We were coming near the bell.

On our right and on our left, enormous red, purple flowers and peonies the colour of blood, and anthuriums like bleeding pleura under the enormous umbrella-like leaves of the petasite plant all seemed to be inclining toward us as we passed and to be ironically showing us the way to the torture. There were also other flowers: flowers of butchery and massacre, tiger-lilies with mutilated necks, diclytrae with their garlands of little red hearts and ferocious labiates with hard, fleshy bodies and mucous tints, like human lips—the lips of my Clara—shouting at us from the tops of their soft stalks:

"Come, my darlings, come more quickly! Where you are going there are still more sufferings, more tortures, more blood running and dripping on to the ground...more twisted, torn bodies groaning on iron tables...more hacked flesh swinging from gibbets...more frightfulness and more hell...come, my loves, come with your lips together and your hands clasped and see the infernal kaleidoscope and devilish feast of death!"

Trembling all over, her teeth clenched, her eyes once again hard and cruel, Clara had fallen silent...She fell silent and as she walked she listened to the voices of the flowers in which she recognised her own voice, her voice of days that were terrible and nights that were murderous, a voice of ferocity, voluptuousness and pain and which not only seemed to come forth from out of the depths of the earth and the depths of death itself but out of the still lower and darker depths of her own soul.

A strident noise, something like the squeaking of a pulley, broke the silence. Then we heard something very soft, and very pure, like the resounding of a crystal cup after it has been hit by a moth in the evening air. We came into a wide, winding path bordered on each side by high trellises which threw their shadows flecked with spots of light on the sand. Clara was avidly looking through the trellises and the leaves. In spite of myself and my sincere resolution to shut my eyes in the face of the accursed scene, I was attracted by that strange magnetism of horror and vanquished by that invincible attraction of the abominable, and I also looked through the trellises and the leaves.

And this is what we saw ...

On the wide, low plateau in a clearing at the end of the gently ascending path, a circular space had been cunningly made into an arbour by skilled gardeners. In the middle of this clearing an enormous, squat bell painted a dull bronze and lugubriously streaked with red patina was suspended from the hook of a pulley on the upper cross piece of a kind of black wooden guillotine with uprights decorated with gilt inscriptions and terrifying masks. Four men, stripped bare to the waist, their muscles tensed and their skin distended until it looked like a mass of deformed humps, were pulling on the cord of the pulley. For all their rhythmically combined efforts, it was all they could do to move and lift the heavy mass of metal which, with every tremor, gave out that almost imperceptible, soft, pure and plaintive sound which we had just heard before its vibrations were lost and died among the flowers. The clapper, a heavy iron pestle, began to oscillate slightly but did not touch the sides of the bell which may have been weary of having tolled the death of some poor devil for so long. Under the dome of the bell, two other men with bare legs and torsos streaming with sweat, their loins girt with a piece of brown cloth, were bending over something we couldn't see ... Their chests with protruding ribs and their lean flanks were giving out a wheezing sound like a spent horse.

All this we could see vaguely, rather confusedly and blurred, between the interstices of the flowers and the lozenges of the trellises, at first in fragments and then in entirety.

"We must hurry!" cried Clara who shut her parasol and boldly lifted her skirts to walk more quickly.

The path still wound ahead of us, sometimes sunny and sometimes in shade, changing at every moment and always mingling ever more inexorable horror with ever more floral beauty.

"Look, my darling!" said Clara ... "Look everywhere ... We're in the most beautiful and interesting part of the garden ... Look at those flowers! Oh those flowers!"

She pointed at strange plants growing in a patch of ground watered from all sides ... I came closer ... Squamiferous and black-spotted like serpents' skins, waving on their tall stalks, I saw enormous spathes like cornets filled with the dark violet of corruption inside and covered outside with the greenish yellow of decomposition ... They were like the open thoraxes of some dead animal ... And from the depths of these cornets there came forth long blood-tinged, sword-shaped tongues like so many monstrous phalluses. Attracted by the corpse-like odour that these horrible plants were exhaling, swarms of flies buzzed around and then disappeared in the depths of each spathe which was carpeted from top to bottom inside with contractile silken hairs which entwined the flies and held them prisoner more surely than any spider's web ... And all along the stalks, finger-like leaves were clenching and twisting like the hands of men being tortured.

"You see, my dear love," said Clara, "these flowers are no creation of a diseased brain or a delirious genius ...

119

Nature made them. I told you that nature loves death!"

"Nature also creates monsters!"

"Monsters! Monsters! First of all, there are no monsters! What you call monsters are forms that are either beyond or outside your imagination ... Are gods not monsters? Isn't a man of genius a monster, like the tiger, the spider or any of those people who live above all social lies in the resplendent and divine immorality of things? But then, I myself am a monster!"

We were now walking between bamboo palisades covered all their length with honeysuckle, sweet-smelling jasmine, begonias, arborescent mallows, and climbing hibiscus not yet in flower. A menisperm was strangling a stone column with its innumerable lianas. At the top of the pillar was the grimacing face of a hideous divinity with ears spreading out like bats' wings and hair ending in spirals of flames. Incarvilleas, day-lilies, nightshade and delphiniums hid the base which was lost among their pink convulvoli, their scarlet thyrsus, their golden calyxes and their purplish stars. An ulcerous, vermin-eaten mendicant bonze who seemed to be the guardian of this place and who was training mongooses from Turan to make somersaults hurled insults at us when he saw us ...

"Dogs! ... Dogs! ... Dogs! ..."

We had to throw a few coins at this maniac whose insults surpassed anything the most filthy imagination could conceive in the way of outrageous obscenities.

"I know him!" said Clara. "He's like the priests of all religions : he wants to frighten us into giving him a little money but he's not a bad devil!"

Here and there in the recesses in the palisade, arranged like rooms full of greenery with beds of flowers, I could see wooden benches armed with chains and bronze collars, cross-shaped iron tables, headsman's blocks and racks, gibbets and machines for automatically quartering bodies, beds strewn with cutting blades and bristling with iron needles, stocks, whipping-posts, wheels, cauldrons and basins over extinguished braziers, and a whole panoply of instruments of sacrifice and torture amid patches of blood, sometimes dry and blackened, and sometimes sticky and red. Hollows in the ground were filled with pools of blood and long tears of blood streaked the sides of dismantled assemblies of torture . . . All around these machines the ground was still bubbling with blood. Specks of blood were staining the whiteness of jasmines and flecking the coral pink of honeysuckle and the mauve of passion-flowers while little morsels of human flesh which had been sent flying by the blows of whips and leather thongs were hanging here and there from the tips of petals and leaves . . . Seeing that I was weakening and flinching from the pools of blood which were spreading to the centre of the pathway, Clara encouraged me in her soft voice :

"It's nothing yet, my darling . . . Come on !"

But it was difficult to go on. The plants, the trees, the air and the ground were full of flies, drunken insects, fierce, fighting coleoptera and gorged mosquitoes. All the fauna of corpses hemmed us in there, by myriads, in the sun . . . Vile larvae were swarming in the red pools or falling in soft clusters from the branches . . . The sand seemed to be breathing or walking, stirring with the seething of vermicular life. We were deafened and blinded and at every instant we were stopped by all these humming swarms of multiplying insects whose every bite would be deadly for Clara, I feared . . . Every now and again we had the horrible feeling that our feet were sinking in the drenched ground as though it had been raining blood !

"It's still nothing . . ." said Clara again. "Let's go on !"

As though to complete the horror of the scene, human faces appeared . . . Teams of workmen were nonchalantly cleaning and repairing the torture instruments as the time for executions in the garden was over for the day . . . They stared at us, no doubt because they were astonished at that time of day and in that place to see two human beings still standing, still living and still with their heads, arms and legs ... A little further on, we saw a pot-bellied and jovial potter squatting on the ground like some China figurine, glazing newly fired flower pots; near him, a basket-maker was plaiting supple reeds and rice straws with his indolent yet precise fingers, making ingenious shelters for plants. A gardener was sharpening his knife on a mill-stone while singing popular airs while an old woman was chewing betel leaves and wagging her head as she placidly picked revolting morsels of human flesh from the pointed teeth of some sort of iron jaw. We also saw children killing rats with sticks and throwing their carcasses into baskets and all along the palisades there were peacocks, famished and ferocious, training the imperial splendour of their mantle of feathers in the blood-covered mud, pecking in their herds at the blood-spattered flowers or crowing like scavengers as they seized strips of flesh sticking to the foliage.

The foetid odour of the slaughterhouse persisted and dominated over all other smells, making us feel sick and retch with irresistible nausea. Even Clara, the fairy queen of scavengers and charnel houses, the angel of decomposition and rottenness, had paled slightly, perhaps because her nerves had failed to sustain her ... Beads of sweat appeared on her brow ... I saw her eyes roll in their sockets and her legs shake.

"I'm cold!" she said.

She looked at me with genuine distress. Her nostrils, always flaring like sails filled with the wind of Death, had contracted and I thought she was about to faint.

"Clara!" I beseeched her. "You see that it's impossible . . . there's a degree of horror that even you can't go beyond . . ."

I held out my arms to her but she pushed them away and straightened herself to face the evil with all the indomitable energy of her frail body.

"Are you mad?" she exclaimed. "Come quickly, my darling . . . quickly !"

Even so, she took out her phial of smelling-salts and breathed deeply . . .

"It's you who are pale and walking like a drunken man . . . I'm not ill . . . I'm quite all right and I feel like singing .. . . "

She began to sing :

Her garments are summer gardens.
And . . .

But she had overestimated her strength and her voice suddenly choked in her throat. I thought the time ripe for bringing her back, for moving or even terrifying her, and vigorously tried to pull her towards me.

"Clara ! My little Clara ! You mustn't abuse your strength or your soul . . . Come back, I beg you !"

But she protested :

"No . . . no . . . let me go . . . don't say anything . . . it's nothing . . . I'm happy !"

She quickly tore herself away from me.

"You see ! . . . There isn't even any blood on my shoes . . . "

And then, in a more irritable tone :

"God ! How tiresome those flies are ! And why don't you try to shut up those horrible peacocks ?"

I tried to chase them away. A few obstinately remained at their sanguinary gleaning task; others clumsily flew off with strident cries and perched near us on the top of the palisades or in the trees where their tails fell down to the ground like so many flowing silks embroidered with dazzling gems . . .

"Filthy beasts !" said Clara.

Thanks to the salts whose cordial emanations she had long been breathing and thanks above all to her implacable determination not to faint, the pink had come back to her complexion and her legs had recovered their swift, nervous energy. In a stronger voice she began to sing again :

> Her garments are summer gardens
> And temples on a feast day
> And her hard swelling breasts shine like two golden vases filled with intoxicating liquors and heady perfumes.
> I have three mistresses . . .

There was a moment's silence and then she began to sing again in a stronger voice which drowned the buzzing of the insects :

> The hair of the third is plaited and coiled on her head
> And never has it known the sweetness of perfumed oils.
> Her face full of passion is deformed
> Her body is like that of a pig . . .
> Always she grunts and she grumbles . . .
> Her breasts and womb exhale the odour of fish.
> She is dirty in her person . . .
> And her bed is more repulsive that the nest of the crow.
> And it is she I love.
> And it is she I love for there is something more mysteriously attractive than beauty and that is divine corruption.
> Corruption in which the eternal fire of life resides.
> And which elaborates the eternal renewal of meta-morphoses !
> I have three mistresses.

And while she sang, while her voice trailed away amid the horrors of the garden, a cloud appeared high, very high, in the sky ... In the immensity of the heavens it was like a tiny little pink ship, a tiny little ship with silken sails that grew as it gently slid onwards.

When Clara had finished singing she had become quite joyous again.

"Oh, the little cloud!" she cried. "Look how pretty and pink it is in the blue! Don't you know it? Haven't you ever seen it? But it's a mysterious little cloud and maybe it isn't a little cloud at all ... Every day, at the same time, it appears from no one knows where ... it's always on its own, always pink ... It glides along, gliding ... gliding ... And then it thins out and melts away in the firmament ... It's gone! And no one knows where it has gone either! There are very learned astronomers here who think it is a genii but I think it's a soul voyaging ... a poor little wandering soul like my own ..."

As though to herself she added:

"And if it were the soul of poor Annie?"

For several minutes she contemplated the unknown cloud which was already growing paler and gradually dissipating.

"Look! There it is melting away ... it's gone! No more little cloud! It's gone!"

She remained wrapt in silent enchantment, her gaze lost in the sky.

A slight breeze had arisen and was gently stirring the trees. The sun was less harsh and overwhelming; its rays were becoming a magnificent copper colour in the west and in the east had softened into the lustrous grey tones and infinite nuances of mother-of-pearl. The shadows of the kiosks, the great trees and the stone Buddhas were turning blue, growing more slender and lengthening on the lawns ...

We were near the bell.
Our view was impeded by tall trunks of plum-trees

125

planted close together but we could guess its whereabouts by the greater shade between the leaves and between the flowers which were white and round like daisies.

The peacocks which had been following us boldly yet prudently, a few yards behind us, their necks craned forward, were spreading their splendid spotted tails on the ground. Some were quite white, with the white of velvet and specks of blood on their breasts, with cruel heads crowned by the diadems of a large fanshaped tuft in which every plume ended in a point like a trembling sliver of pink crystal.

Iron tables, racks and sinister devices multiplied before our eyes. In the shade of a giant tamarisk we saw a kind of rococo armchair. The arm-rests were made alternately of a saw and a razor-sharp blade of steel while the back-rest and seat consisted of a mass of iron spikes. A scrap of flesh was hanging from one spike. Clara lightly and skil-fully lifted it up at the end of her umbrella and threw it to the voracious peacocks who rushed forward with wings beating and fought over it furiously. For a few minutes there was such a dazzling mêlée and clash of brilliant jewel-like colours that despite all my disgust I tarried to admire the marvellous sight. Perched in the neighbouring trees, lophophores, sacred pheasants and Malayan fight-ing-cocks with damascened breasts were watching the merry-go-round of the peacocks and slyly awaiting the hour of their feast.

All of a sudden, a large opening, a kind of arch of light and flowers appeared before us in the wall of plum-trees and there before us, enormous and terrifying, was the bell . . . The heavy framework holding it was varnished with black, decorated with gilt inscriptions and red masks, and it shone strangely in the sun like some temple. All around, the ground was strewn with sand to deaden all sounds, and surrounded by the flowering plum-trees covered from top to bottom of their trunks with their white bouquets of blossom. In the midst of this red and white circus the bell was a sinister sight. It was like a pit or abyss suspended in the air and seeming to rise towards the sky, its inner depths lost in dumb darkness.

It was at that moment that we understood what it was that the two thin-waisted men with brown loin-cloths, whom we had seen under the bell as we came into the garden, were bending over. They were bending over a corpse which they were freeing from the cords and leather thongs with which they had solidly fastened it. The corpse was the colour of ochre clay, completely naked and lying face downwards. The body was dreadfully contracted, its muscles bulging, its skin a mass of uneven swellings and depressions, like tumours. We could see that the victim had long struggled and vainly tried to break his bonds and that his desperate and ceaseless efforts had gradually made the cords and leather thongs sink into his flesh where they now were rimmed with streaks of brown blood, congealed pus and greenish tissue. With one foot on the corpse, their backs bent, their two arms stretched like cables, the men were pulling at the thongs which they could only pull away by tearing off strips of flesh ... From their throats there issued a rhythmic panting which soon ended in a hoarse wheezing ...

We came closer ...

The peacocks had stopped still. Their numbers swelled, they now crowded the circular path behind the flowered opening that they did not dare to pass. Behind us we could hear their cries and their shuffling tread like that of a crowd which had run to the threshold of a temple and which was standing there respectfully, eyes round with amazement, staring at a mystery they could not understand.

We came still closer.

"Look, darling," said Clara, "and see how curious and unique it all is. How magnificent! In what other country would you find such a sight? A torture chamber decked out as though for a ball and with a dazzling throng of peacocks to serve as attendants, people and guests! Wouldn't you say that we were being transported out of this life into the poetry and fantasies of old legends? Really, aren't you astonished? It always seems to me here that I'm living in a dream!"

Pheasants with brilliant plumage and long golden tails were flying across each other's paths above our heads. Several boldly perched here and there on the tops of the blossoming trees.

Clara followed every caprice of these fairy-like flights, every changing pattern of form and colour. After a few minutes of enchanted silence she spoke again :

"See my love what astonishing people the Chinese really are even though they are so despised by those who don't know them! No other people has been able to tame nature with such a precise intelligence... What unique artists they are! And what poets! Look at that corpse on the red sand with its hues of old idols... Look at it well for it's extraordinary... You would think that the vibrations of the bell, when rung at full peal, had pierced into the body like sharp knives... that they had pulled up the muscles, cracked the veins and twisted and crushed the bones... A simple sound, so gentle to the ear, so delightfully musical and so moving to the soul, becoming something a thousand times more terrible and painful than all the complicated instruments of that fat old clown! Don't you think it's astounding? Really, to think of such a marvel... to think that the bell which makes amorous virgins weep with ecstasy and divine melancholy as they walk in the evening countryside can also make a miserable human carcass roar with suffering and even die in the most unspeakable pain... I think it's pure genius... Oh what a wonderful torture! And how discreet it is since it's accomplished in the dark! When you think of it it's horror can be compared to no other ... But like the torture of the caress, it's very rare today and you're very lucky to have seen it on your first visit to the garden ... They tell me that the Chinese brought it from Korea where it is a very ancient torture and still frequently used ... We'll go to Korea if you like ... the Koreans are torturers of unparalleled ferocity ... And yet they make the most beautiful vases in the world—vases that are quite unique, with a thick white glaze, vases which are said to have been dipped—oh, if only you knew!—in baths of seminal fluid!"

Then, coming back to the corpse :

"I would like to know who this man is! They only order the torture of the bell here for criminals of quality : conspiring princes and high dignitaries who no longer have the Emperor's favour ... It's an aristocratic and almost glorious torture ... "

She shook my arm :

"What I'm saying doesn't seem to excite you ... And you're not even listening to me! But just think of it ... This bell when it's rung ... It's so gentle! when you hear it from afar it makes you think of mystical Easter rites, joyful masses ... baptisms and marriages ... And yet it's the most terrifying of deaths! I find that wonderful! And what about you?"

But as I didn't reply :

"Yes, yes," she insisted, "say that it's wonderful! I want you to! Be kind to me!"

But as I persisted in my silence, she made a little movement of anger.

"How disagreeable you are!" she said. "You're never kind to me! What can we find to cheer you? Oh, I don't want to love you any more ... I've no more desire for you ... Tonight you'll lie all alone in the kiosk and I'll go to find my little Peach-Flower who is much nicer that you are and who knows how to make love much better than men . . .

I was about to stammer something but she stopped me :

"No! No! Let me go! It's finished! I don't want to speak to you any more . . . And I'm sorry not to have brought Peach-Flower with me . . . You're unbearable. You make me sad . . . You make me stupid . . . It's odious! And now I've wasted a day which I thought would be so exciting with you!"

Her chattering and her voice irritated me. For the last few moments I had no longer seen her beauty. Her eyes, her lips, her neck, her heavy golden hair, even the fires of her desire and the lusts of her sin, everything in her now seemed hideous to me. From her open corsage, from the pink nudity of her bosom where I had so often breathed, drunk and bitten in the intoxication of her heady perfumes, there now arose the exhalations of putrefying flesh—that little mass of putrefying flesh which was her soul . . . Several times, I was tempted to interrupt her with some violent, outrageous gesture . . . to shut her mouth with my fist . . . to wring her neck . . . I felt such a savage hatred surging up in me against this woman that I roughly seized her arm and cried in a demented voice :

"Be quiet! Be quiet, will you! Never speak to me again, never! I could kill you, you devil! I should kill you and throw you to the carrion, you carrion-crow!"

Despite my fury I was afraid of my own words. But to make them finally irremediable, I repeated them while I crushed her arm with my murderous hands :

"Carrion! Carrion! Carrion!"

Clara neither recoiled nor flickered one eyelid . . . She bent forward and offered her throat to me . . . Her face lit up with an unknown, shining joy. Simply, slowly and with infinite gentleness, she said to me :

"Well, then! Kill me, darling . . . I'd love to be killed by you, dear little heart!"

There had been a lightning flash of rebellion in the

dark of my long and painful passive submission. No sooner had it flared up than it went out. Ashamed of what I had shouted and of my ignoble insults I let go Clara's arm and all my anger, due to nervous excitation, suddenly melted away into a great calm.

"Ah, you see!" said Clara, who did not wish to exult overmuch in my pitiful defeat and her too easy triumph, "you haven't even got the courage . . . It would have been wonderful . . . poor child!"

And as if nothing had passed between us then, she again gazed with passionate interest at the frightful drama being enacted with the bell.

During this short scene, the two men had been resting. They seemed exhausted. Thin and panting, with their ribs protruding under their skin, and their thighs bone-thin, they hardly seemed human any more . . . Sweat was streaming from the points of their moustaches and their chests were heaving like those of wild animals cornered by dogs. But a supervisor appeared suddenly, whip in hand. He shouted some angry words and then lashed the bony thighs of the two wretches who resumed their task with screams . . .

Frightened by the cracking of the whip, the peacocks started to scream and beat their wings. They fled in a tumult and then, gradually reassured, came back one by one, couple by couple, group by group, and regained their place under the flowery arch where they displayed the splendour of their breasts and gazed ever more ferociously at the scene of death. The red, yellow and blue-hued pheasants were still wheeling over the white ring and embroidering the luminous ceiling of the sky with their brilliant silken colours and changing patterns.

Clara called the supervisor and engaged in a brief con-

"These are the two poor devils who've been ringing the versation with him in Chinese, translating for me as he answered.

bell ... Forty-two hours without eating or drinking, without one rest! Would you believe it? And why aren't they dead too? I know that the Chinese aren't like us and that they have an extraordinary endurance of fatigue and physical pain ... I once wanted to see how long a Chinese could work without eating . . . Twelve days, darling—he only fell down at the end of the twelfth day! It's unbelievable! It's true that the work I made him do wasn't comparable with what we're seeing ... I only made him dig the ground under the sun ... "

She had forgotten my insults, her voice had become loving and caressing again as though she were telling me some beautiful love story. She went on :

"You can imagine, my darling, what violent, continuous, superhuman efforts are needed to swing and peal the bell? many—even the strongest—collapse under the strain ...A burst vein...a rupture and that's it! They drop dead under the bell and those who don't die on the spot fall incurably sick! Look how the rubbing of the rope has made their hands swollen and bleeding! Besides, it seems that they're victims as well! They die as they kill and one execution leads to another! Never mind, we must be good to these wretches ... when the supervisor has gone you will give them a few *taels* won't you?"

She went over to the corpse.

"Oh! I know him now ... He's a rich banker from the city. He was very rich and robbed everybody ... But it wasn't for that that he was sentenced to the torture of the bell. The supervisor doesn't know quite why ... They say he was betraying his country to the Japanese ... they have to say something ... "

Hardly had she finished speaking than we heard the sound of stifled laments and sobs. They came from opposite us, behind the white wall from which petals were falling slowly to the red sand ... A rain of tears and flowers!

"It's the family," explained Clara, "they're there by

custom, waiting to be given the body of the victim."

At that moment, the two exhausted executioners made a supreme last effort while they were still standing and turned over the corpse. Clara and I both cried out in unison. She pressed herself close to me and tore my shoulder with her nails, crying:

"Oh, darling! Darling! Darling!"

In her exclamations she still expressed all the intensity of her emotions that reacted to terror as though to love.

We looked at the corpse with the same thunderstruck gaze. We both stared and stared and could not take our eyes away from it.

On its convulsed face, with tensed muscles stretched in a frightful grimace amid the hollows and hideous angles of the countenance, the mouth was twisted open to reveal gums and teeth in an unspeakably frightful, demented grin—a grin frozen by death which had modelled it out of all the furrows of the skin. The two eyes were open unnaturally wide and gazed at us with a look that was unseeing but still full of the most terrifying madness—a face of such prodigiously grinning, such demented madness that never in any lunatic asylum have I ever seen a more terrifying expression in the eyes of any living madman.

As I looked at the body and noticed all its muscular displacements, all its twisted tendons, protruding bones and its frightful grin, and all the madness that lingered even after death in its eyes I understood that the agony of this man who had lain for forty-two hours in his bonds under the bell must have been worse than the agony of any other torture in the world. Neither the knife that dismembers, piece by piece, the red-hot iron that burns, the pincers that tear or the racks and wooden joints that dislocate members, crack articulations and crush bones like so many pieces of wood could effect worse ravages on the organs of a living body or fill a brain with more frightful nightmares and terror that than this invisible and immaterial tolling of a bell—a bell that had become worse than every known instrument of torture, and which attacked every sensitive part of the body at the same time and accomplished the work of more than a hundred tor- turers ...

The two men had begun again to pull at the thongs, with their throats whistling and their sides heaving ever more quickly. But their strength was failing and ran out of their bodies in streams of sweat. It was all they could do to keep themselves erect and clasp the leather thongs with their stiffening, sprained fingers ...

"Dogs!" shrieked the supervisor.

A whiplash curled around their loins but they did not even react against the pain. It seemed that all feeling had gone from their overworked nerves. Their knees bent even more, shook and knocked together. All that remained of their muscles under their flayed skin contracted in tetanic spasms. All of a sudden, one of them came to the end of his tether, let go of the thongs, uttered a low harsh cry and fell with arms upflung near the corpse, his face to the ground, vomiting a flood of black blood.

"Up you scum! Up you dog!" cried the supervisor.

Four times his lash whistled through the air and tore at the man's back. The pheasants perching on the flowered trees flew away with a great beating of wings. Behind us I could hear the panic-stricken cries of the peacocks. But the man did not get up ... He no longer moved while the pool of blood widened on the sand. He was dead!

I then dragged Clara away even though her fingers were digging into my skin. I felt I had become very pale and I was walking and staggering like a drunkard.

"It's too much ... it's too much!" I kept on saying while Clara, who was meekly following me, said:

"Ah! You see, my darling! I knew it! Have I lied to you?"

We came to a path which led us to the central pond

134

while the peacocks that had hitherto been following us suddenly left us and noisily departed among the bushes and lawns of the garden.

This path was a very wide one and bordered with dead trees, huge tamarind-trees whose thick, denuded branches were interlacing in angular arabesques against the sky. A niche had been dug in each tree-trunk. Although most niches were empty, some contained the bodies of violently contorted men and women who had been subjected to hideous and obscene tortures. In front of each occupied niche, a kind of registrar in a black robe was standing with an air of great solemnity and a legal register in his hands, pressed against his belly.

"It's the path of the accused..." Clare told me. "All these people you see standing here are waiting to gather the confessions that prolonged suffering might tear from these wretches. They rarely confess since they prefer to die like this rather than drag out their last days in the cages of the prison and finally perish in other torments. The tribunals don't generally abuse their powers of preventive arrest except in the case of political crimes. They judge people in handfuls, at random... Anyway, you can see that there aren't many detainees and that most niches are empty. But the idea is still ingenious. I do believe that it comes from Greek mythology. For all its horror, it's only a transposition of that charming fable of the hamadryads who were captives of the trees!"

Clara went up to a tree in which a young woman was groaning. She was hanging by the wrists from an iron hook and her wrists had been imprisoned by a wooden vice which was tightly screwed while a rough cord made of coconut filaments and covered with powdered pimento and mustard was tightly wound around her arms.

"The cord is kept tight," Clara explained to me, "until the limbs are swollen to four times their natural size. Then it's taken off and the ulcers it produces often burst into hideous open wounds. People often die from them and no cure is possible".

"But supposing the detainee is proved innocent?" I asked.

"Well then—it's too bad!" said Clara.

In another niche there was another woman with legs held apart until she was almost quartered. Her neck and arms were held in iron collars ... Her eyelids, nostrils, lips and sexual parts had been rubbed with red pepper and the nipples of her breasts were squeezed between two vices ... Further on, a young man was hanging from a rope running under his two armpits; a large piece of stone was fastened to his shoulders and we could hear the cracking of his joints ... Another, pulled forward by a brass wire fastened to his neck and toes, was squatting with sharp, pointed stones between the folds of his thighs ... the niches in the trees were becoming emptier. It was only occasionally that I saw a bound, crucified or hanging prisoner who might have been sleeping or dead! Clara spoke no longer, and explained no more ... She was listening to the flapping of vultures who were passing above the interlacing branches above us and, to the crowing of ravens who were hovering higher still, in innumerable flocks ...

The lugubrious alley of tamarind-trees led to a large terrace covered with peonies and it was from there that we went down to the pond ...

The long stems of iris soared out of the water, bearing their extraordinary flowers with petals coloured like old potsherds; precious emeralds with violet tints, streaked with the hues of blood; sinister purples, blues with flame-like tints of orange ochre; velvety blacks with specks of sulphur ... A few of the largest and most contorted plants looked like Cabbalistic characters ... Water-lilies and nelumbiums were floating on the golden water and their great blossoms reminded me of so many decapitated, floating heads . . . We stayed there for a few minutes, bending over the balustrade, silently gazing at the water. An enormous carp, only his golden head visible, was sleeping under a leaf and gold-fish were darting between the lilies and the reeds like red thoughts in the inflamed mind of a woman.

And so the day ended.

The sky became red, streaked with wide purplish streaks of surprising translucence. It was the hour when the flowers took on a mysterious brilliance, and their radiance became both violent and restrained . . . Everywhere they were aflame as though they were giving back to the evening air all the light and sun they had imbibed during the day. The paths strewn with powdered brick were like ribbons of fire or streams of incandescent lava between the strident green of the lawns. The birds fell silent in the trees while the insects ceased buzzing to die or fall asleep. Only the nocturnal butterflies and bats began to wheel through the air. From the sky to the trees, from the trees to the ground, everywhere, silence descended upon the garden. I felt it penetrating into my being and laying its cold touch on me, like death.

A flock of cranes slowly descended the grassy slope and lined up in a row around the pond, not far from us. I could hear the rustling of their claws in the tall grass and the sharp clicking of their beaks. As they stood on one leg, motionless, their heads tucked under their wings, you would have said they were so many bronze statues. The golden headed carp who had been sleeping under a nelumbium leaf suddenly dived and disappeared into the depths of the pond, amid a ripple of little waves which softly rocked the closed calyxes of the water-lilies and then became lost amid tufts of irises whose strangely simplified but diabolical flowers wrote fatalistic signs from the book of destinies in the magic of the evening . . .

137

An enormous, flaring carnivorous orchid was waving the cone of its greenish, brown-flecked flower above the water and sent us its strong smell of death. For a long time the flies buzzed round the charnel-house of its calyx with unrelenting persistence and obstinacy . . .

Her elbows leaning on the balustrade, her brow darkened, her eyes staring, Clara gazed at the water. A ray of the setting sun set her neck ablaze . . . Her body had become more relaxed and her lips had become thinner. She was solemn and very sad. She was looking at the water but her gaze went further and deeper than the water; she was gazing, perhaps, into something even blacker and more impenetrable than the water of the pond—into her soul perhaps, the abyss of her soul in which the monstrous flowers of her desire were writhing amid flames and blood . . . What was she really looking at? What was she thinking of? I did not know . . . She may have been looking at nothing . . . thinking of nothing . . . Slightly weary, her nerves broken and wounded by the whiplashes of too many sins, she was simply keeping silence . . . Unless, by some last effort of her mind, she was gathering all the souvenirs and images of this day of horror to make an offering of a bouquet of red flowers to her sex? I did not know . . .

I did not dare speak to her. She frightened me and also disturbed me to my very depths by her immobility and her silence. Did she really exist? I wondered to myself, not without fear . . . Could she not have been born out of my debaucheries and my fever? Was she not one of those impossible images that a nightmare can engender? One of those criminal temptations born by lust in the diseased minds of murderers and madmen? Could she not be my soul, issued forth from my body against my will and materialising itself into the shape of sin?

But no . . . I touched her. My hand recognised the admirable reality, the living truth of her body . . . through

the thin, silken dress which covered her, her skin burned
my fingers . . . Clara did not tremble at the touch of my
hand; she did not swoon under its caress as she had so
often done in the past. I desired her and yet I hated
her . . . I wanted to take her in my arms and hold her
tight until I choked her, until I crushed her, until I had
drunk death—her death—from her open veins. In a tone
at once menacing and abject, I cried out to her :

"Clara ! . . . Clara ! . . . Clara !"

She did not reply or move . . . She looked at the darken-
ing water . . . I think, in truth, that she was looking neither
at the water, nor at the red reflections of the sky in the
water, neither at the flowers nor at herself . . . then, I
moved away so that I could no longer see or touch her
and I turned towards the sun which was disappearing,
that sun of which nothing remained in the sky but a few
ephemeral streaks of light which were gradually melting
away into the darkness of night . . .

The shadows fell upon the garden, mantling it with blue
veils that lay lightly on its lawns and more thickly on the
bushes which were losing the complexity of their shapes.
The white blossoms of the peach and cherry trees now
assumed a truly lunar whiteness and had the gliding, wandering, and strangely stooping aspect of so many
ghosts . . . The sinister cross-pieces and black uprights of
gibbets and gallows stood stark against the steel-blue
eastern sky.

What horror! Above a bush and outlined against the
dying purple of the evening, I could see the black silhouettes of five tortured men turning on stakes or turning,
endlessly turning, in the void like so many huge flowers
dangling from their stalks.

"Clara ! . . . Clara ! . . . Clara !"

But my voice did not reach her. Clara did not reply,
move or turn round. She remained leaning over the water.
And no more than she heard me did she hear the laments,

the cries and the groans of those who were dying in the garden.

I felt within myself a great burden, like an immense weariness after long marches through fever-ridden forests and along the shores of deadly lakes and I was invaded by a feeling of discouragement which, it seemed, would stay with me for ever ... At the same time, my brain felt heavy as lead ... It was as if an iron band was being tightened around my temples until my skull would burst open.

Then, gradually, my thoughts flew away from the garden, the circuses of torture, the agonies of the dying man under the bell, the trees haunted with human suffering and all those blood-stained and devouring flowers ... It was as though my mind wished to leave this charnel house and penetrate into the pure light to knock upon the doors of Life ... Alas! The Doors of Life only open on to death ... only open on to the palaces and gardens of death . . . The whole universe appeared to me as an immense and inexorable garden of tortures ... Everywhere there was blood and where there was most life, there would horrible torturers ravage your flesh, saw your bones and flay your skin, their faces glowing with sinister joy ...

Ah yes, the garden of tortures! ... the passions, appetites, interests, hatreds, lies, laws, social institutions, love, glory, heroism and religions are all the monstrous flowers and hideous instruments of eternal human suffering ... What I saw that day, what I heard, exists and screams and moans beyond this garden which became for me nothing but a symbol for the whole world ... In vain do I seek for a halt to it in crime, or a rest from it in death for I can find rest nowhere ...

I would like ... yes, I would like to cleanse my soul and brain with old memories of known and familiar faces ... I called Europe to my aid with its hypocritical civilisations, and my Paris of pleasure and laughter ... But it was the face of Eugene Mortain I saw grimacing on the shoulders

of the fat and loquacious executioner whom I had seen
sitting amid the flowers at the foot of the gibbet, wiping
his scalpels and saws ... they were the eyes, the mouth,
the flabby, falling cheeks of Madame G*** that I now saw
bending over the racks and her violet-hued hands that I
now saw touching and caressing the iron jaws gorged with
human meat : ... It was on all those I had loved or
thought to have loved, it was on all the judges, soldiers
and priests, everywhere, that the ineffacable red stain of
blood was spreading and it was in the churches, the barracks and the temples of justice that they were furiously
pursuing the task of death ... It was man-the-individual
and man-the-crowd, the wild animal, the plant, the element and the whole of nature that I saw impelled by the
cosmic force of love as they rushed towards murder in the
belief that it was thus that they would find something
beyond life, a glutting of all the furious desires of life that
devoured them and spurted out of life in jets of filthy
foam!

A few moments before, I had been asking myself who
Clara was and if she really existed? But now I knew that
Clara was life, the true presence of life, the whole of life!

"Clara! ... Clara! ... Clara!"

She did not nswer. She neither moved nor turned
round. A denser, blue and silver mist was rising from the
lawns and pond to enwreathe the bushes and blur the
outlines of the torture scaffolds ... It seemed to me that an
odour of blood and of corpses was also rising with it—an
incense offered to the immortal glory of death and the
immortal glory of Clara by invisible censers swung by
invisible hands!

Behind me, at the other end of the pond, the gecko was
beginning to strike the hour ... Another gecko answered ...
then another ... then another, at regular intervals ... They
were like bells calling each other and conversing by means
of song, festival bells with an extraordinarily pure timbre

and a crystal-clear sonority which was so soft that it suddenly dissipated all the nightmare figures that haunted the garden, gave security to silence and the charm of some untroubled dream to the night ... So clear, so inexpressibly clear were the notes of the gecko that they awoke within me thousands upon thousands of nocturnal landscapes in which my lungs could breathe again and in which I could think again ... In a few minutes I had forgotten that I was with Clara and that all around me, the soil and the flowers were oozing blood. I saw myself once again wandering through the silver twilight amid the fairy-like rice-fields of Annam.

"Let's go back!" said Clara.

Her sharp, aggressive, weary voice brought me back to reality. Clara was standing in front of me, leaning on her parasol. I could divine the shape of her crossed legs under the tight folds of her dress. In the penumbra, her lips were glistening like the little veiled glow of a pink screen in a large darkened room.

As I didn't move, she said :

"Well, I'm waiting for you !"

I tried to take her arm but she refused.

"No ... no. Let's walk side by side !"

I insisted.

"You must be tired, dear Clara ... You—"

"No ... no !"

"It's a long way from here to the river. Take my arm, I beg you !"

"No thank you ! Be quiet ! Oh, be quiet !"

"Clara, you aren't the same !"

"If you wish to please me, then be quiet ! I don't want anyone to talk to me at this hour !"

Her voice was sharp, cutting and imperious ... We started to go back ... We crossed the bridge, she in front and I behind and we followed the little paths which snaked across the lawns. Clara was walking with abrupt, painful steps...But such was the invulnerable beauty of her body that even her painful efforts did not break the harmonious, supple and fully-rounded line of her body... Her hips still swayed with a divinely voluptuous undulation...Even when her mind was far from love, even when it was stiffening and protesting against love, it was always love and all the forms and intoxications and ardours of love that were animated and shaped her body...there was not one attitude, not one gesture, not one tremor, not one floating of her hair in the wind and not one rustle of her dress which did not cry out with love, which did not breathe love, and which did not bathe all things and people around her with love. The sand on the pathway seemed to cry out under her little feet and I listened to it as though it were a cry of desire or a kiss in which I could always hear that same name that I had always heard among the creaking of gallows or the death-rattle of dying men—that name which was now resounding through the twilight air like an exquisite and funeral obsession :

"Clara!...Clara!...Clara!"

To hear it better, the gecko had fallen silent. Everything had fallen silent...

The twilight was wonderful. It was one of infinite softness and a caressing freshness which intoxicated me. We were walking amid perfumes...We brushed past marvellous flowers which were even more marvellous since we could barely see them and which inclined and greeted us as we passed like so many mysterious fairies. Nothing of the horror of the garden remained any longer. Only its beauty remained to tremble and exult with us as the night fell ever more deliciously down upon us.

I had pulled myself together. It seemed to me that my fever had gone. My limbs were becoming lighter, more elastic and stronger...While I walked my fatigue dissi-

143

pated itself and I felt something rise in me that was akin to a violent need for love. I drew close to Clara and walked beside her . . . close to her . . . set aflame by her . . . But Clara no longer had the same expression of lust that she had had when she was nibbling the thalicter flower or passionately smearing her lips with its acrid pollen . . . the icy expression on her face belied all the lascivious stirrings of her body . . . As far as I could see when I examined her, it seemed to me that the lust that was in her and which had flamed so strangely in her eyes or moaned through her lips had disappeared as completely from her lips and eyes as the blood-filled images of the tortures in the garden.

I asked her in a voice that trembled :

"Are you cross with me, Clara? Do you hate me?"

She replied crossly :

"But of course not! That's got nothing to do with it! I beg you to be quiet. You don't know how you're tiring me!"

I insisted :

"Yes, yes! I see that you hate me! It's terrible! I could weep . . . "

"God! How you annoy me! Be quiet and cry if you feel like it . . . But be quiet!"

As we were passing the spot where we had stopped to talk with the old executioner, I thought in my stupid obstinacy that I could bring a smile back to Clara's lips by saying to her :

"Do you remember the fat old fellow, my love? How funny he was with his blood-stained robe, his case of instruments, and his red fingers, my darling little heart? And his theories on the sex of flowers? Do you remember? He said that as many as twenty males are needed for one single female to have orgasm?"

This time, a shrug of her shoulders was my only answer. She no longer deigned even to show anger at my words.

144

Then, impelled by a coarse access of lust, I clumsily leaned over towards her, tried to put my arm around her waist, and brutally took hold of her breasts.

"I want you . . . here . . . you understand . . . in this garden . . . in this silence . . . at the foot of these gibbets . . ."

I was panting, a vile slaver was dribbling from my lips and a flow of abominable words—the words that she loved to hear!

With a sudden twist of her body, Clara freed herself from my heavy, clumsy grasp and in a voice in which there was anger, irony and weariness as well as irritation, she said :

"My God! What a bore you are! My poor friend, if only you knew how ridiculous you are! You filthy animal! Take your hands off me! Later on, if you like, you can get rid of your filthy lusts with the harlots . . . Really, you're too ridiculous for words!"

Ridiculous! yes, I could feel myself to be ridiculous and I decided to remain quiet. I no longer wished to break her silence like a great stone plunging into a lake where swans are sleeping in the moonlight!

The sampan, lit with red lanterns, was waiting for us at the jetty beside the prison. A Chinese woman with a weatherbeaten face, dressed in a blouse and black silk trousers, with bare arms loaded with heavy golden spangles and large gold rings in her ears, was holding the hawser. Clara leapt on board and I followed her.

"Where must I take you?" the woman asked Clara in English.

Clara replied in a jerky, somewhat trembling voice :

"Where you like . . . anywhere . . . on the river . . . you know it well . . . "

I saw then that she was very pale. Her pinched nostrils, her drawn features and glazed eyes all expressed suffering. The Chinese woman nodded.

"Yes, yes, I know."

She had thick lips eaten by betel juice, and a look of bestial hardness. She muttered some words that I did not understand.

"Come, Ki-Pai," Clara ordered sharply, "be quiet and do what I tell you. Anyway, the gates of the city are shut."

"The gates of the garden are open."

"Do as I say."

Letting go of the hawser, the Chinese deftly grabbed hold of the stern-oar and skilfully began to manoeuvre it. We slid over the water.

The night was soft. We were breathing a tepid but infinitely light night air ... The water was singing below the bows of the sampan and the river was lit as though for a great festival.

On the other bank, to our right and to our left, we could see lanterns of every colour lighting the masts, sails and crowded decks of boats. A strange clamour of cries, songs and music came to us over the water as though from a rejoicing crowd. The water was a velvety black, lit here and there with dull shimmering patches of light and with no other reflections than the red and green reflections of the lanterns decorating the sampans which were crisscrossing the river in all directions ... Through the darkness and under a dark sky we could see the storied terraces of the city glowing like an immense red brazier between the black silhouettes of trees, like a mountain of fire.

As we moved away, we could vaguely see the high walls of the prison with watchmen and turning searchlights throwing their triangles of blinding light on the river and on the countryside.

Clara had gone under the baldaquin which made the boat into a kind of soft, silk-lined boudoir redolent of love. Strong perfumes were burning in a very ancient forged iron vase roughly shaped as an elephant, with its four squat and massive feet resting among a delicate tracery of roses. The hangings were decorated with voluptuous prints with scenes of bold lust strangely executed by the cunning hand of a great artist. The frieze of the baldaquin, a precious piece of carved and painted wood, was the exact reproduction of a fragment of decoration from the underground temple of Elephanta which archaeologists, according to the Brahmin tradition, have puritanically called: the Union of the Crow. A wide, thick mattress of embroidered silk filled the centre of the boat and from the roof there hung a lantern with phallic shaped windows, partly covered with orchids so that the interior of the sampan had the mysterious half-light of a sanctuary or a lovers' boudoir.

Clara threw herself down upon the cushions. She was extraordinarily pale and her body shook with nervous spasms. I wanted to take her hands . . . They were ice-cold.

"Clara! Clara!" I implored her, "what's the matter? What is the matter with you? Speak to me!"

She replied in a husky voice which seemed to be coming with pain from the depths of her contracted throat:

"Leave me alone . . . Don't touch me . . . Don't say anything . . . I'm ill . . ."

Her pallor, her bloodless lips and her voice which sounded like a death-rattle frightened me. I thought she was about to die. Panic-stricken, I called the Chinese woman:

"Quickly! Quickly! Clara is dying!"

But after drawing the curtains aside and showing her chimaera-like face, Ki-Pai shrugged her shoulders and brutally cried:

"It's nothing! She's always like that each time she comes back from that place."

And muttering, she went back to her oar.

Impelled by the nervous arms of Ki-Pai, the boat skimmed forth over the river. We passed other sampans similar

to our own, with baldaquins with drawn curtains through which I could hear songs, the sound of kisses, laughter and the moans of love mingling with the splashing of the water and the far-off, stifled sounds of tom-toms and gongs...
In a few minutes we had reached the far bank but we spent a long time sailing alongside black and deserted or lit and crowded landing-stages, low-class hovels, tea-houses for the sentries and flower-boats for the sailors and all the scum of the port. Through the port-holes and lit windows I could only barely glimpse rapid visions of strangely daubed faces, lewd dances, screaming debauches and faces made evil with opium...

Clara remained insensible to all that was happening around her as she lay in the silken bark on the river. Her face was buried in a cushion which she was biting with her teeth... I tried to make her breathe smelling salts. Three times, she waved the flask away with a weary gesture. Her bosom bare, her two breasts bursting out of the torn silk of her corsage, her legs as taut and quivering as a violin string, she was breathing painfully. I did not know what to say or do... I bent over her with anguish in my soul, full of tragic uncertainty and troubled premonitions... To assure myself that it was only a temporary crisis and that the springs of life were still intact in her I seized her wrists. I could feel her pulse beating as lightly, as rapidly and as regularly as the little heart of a child or a bird. Now and again she sighed—a long and painful sigh that swelled her pink bosom... I gently murmured:

"Clara!... Clara!... Clara!"

She neither heard nor saw me, and remained with her face buried in the cushion. Her hat had slipped off her hair whose russet gold took on the colour of old mahogany under the light of the lamp and her two feet clad in silk moccasins peeped forth from her dress and showed stains of blood mixed with mud.

"Clara!... Clara!... Clara!"

148

Nothing to be heard except the song of the waters and far-off music; nothing to be seen except the burning mountain of the terrible city, through the curtains of the baldaquin and, nearer, red, green, undulating reflections like luminous eels sinking into the black river.

There was a bump... A call from the Chinese woman ... We moored by a kind of long illuminated terrace full of the noise of music and feasting like one of the flower-boats.

Ki-Pai fastened the boat to iron rings in front of a staircase with red steps that went down into the water. Two enormous round lanterns were shining from the top of masts decorated with yellow streamers.

"Where are we?" I asked.

"Where she ordered me to take you," replied Ki-Pai gruffly. "We are where she comes to pass the night when she comes back from over there."

I suggested :

"Wouldn't it be better to take her back home seeing her state of suffering?"

Ki-Pai answered :

"She's always like this after the prison ... And then, the city is closed and to get to the palace by the gardens is too far now and too dangerous."

She added, scornfully :

"She's very well looked after here. Here, they know her !"

"Help me then," I ordered, "and don't be rough with her."

Very gently and carefully, Ki-Pai and I lifted Clara in our arms and half-carrying her, half-supporting her, we managed to get her out of the boat and up the stairs. She weighed heavily on us and was ice-cold. Her head fell back slightly and her completely dishevelled hair fell in burnished waves over her shoulders. With one hand feebly clasping Ki-Pai, she was uttering faint little moans and disjointed words like a child. Panting under her weight, I groaned :

"My God ! I hope she isn't dying . . . not dying !"

Ki-Pai sniggered fiercely :

"Dying ! She ! It isn't suffering she's got in her body—it's filth !"

We were welcomed at the top of the staircase by two women with painted eyes. Their golden nudity could be seen in its entirety under the light, vaporous veils draping them. They wore obscene jewels in their hair, bracelets around their wrists, fingers and ankles, and their skin had been rubbed with delicate essences which exhaled the perfumes of a garden.

One of them clapped her hands with joy.

"But it's our little friend ! I told you that she would be coming, the dear heart . . . .. she always comes . . . Quick . . . quick . . . lay her on the bed, the poor love !"

She pointed at a kind of mattress or stretcher placed along the wall. We laid Clara on it. She was no longer moving. Although her eyelids were opened frighteningly wide, all we could see of her eyes were two white globes. The Chinese girl with painted eyes then bent over Clara and in a delightfully rhythmic voice, as though she were singing, she said :

"Little, little mistress of my breasts and my soul . . . how beautiful you are too ! You are as beautiful as a young dead girl and yet you're not dead . . . You will live again, little mistress, from my lips and under my caresses and the perfumes of my mouth."

She dabbed Clara's temples with a strong perfume and made her smell salts

"Yes, yes, darling little mistress, you have fainted and you can't hear me ! You can't feel the softness of my fingers but your heart is beating . . . beating . . . And love is galloping in your veins like a young horse . . . love bounds in your veins like a young tiger."

150

She turned towards me.

"You mustn't be sad because she always faints when she comes here... In a few minutes we shall be crying with pleasure in her happy, burning flesh ... "

I stood there inert and silent, my limbs as heavy as lead, my chest constricted as though in a nightmare ... I no longer had any feeling of reality ... Everything that I saw—blurred images arising out of the surrounding darkness or the depths of the river, only falling back into darkness to reappear once more with fantastic deformations—terrified me... the long terrace that seemed to be suspended in the night air, with its red lacquer balustrades, its slender columns supporting its boldly curving roof, its garlands of lanterns alternating with garlands of flowers, was thronged with a chattering, lively and extraordinarily colourful crowd. A hundred pairs of painted eyes were staring at us and a hundred painted mouths were saying something I could not hear but which seemed me to be always the same refrain :

"Clara! Clara! Clara!"

Naked and entwined bodies, tattooed arms covered with golden bracelets, bellies and breasts were all whirling round and round amid a mass of flying scarves. And in the midst of it all, around it all, over and beyond it all, there were cries, laughter, songs, the sounds of flutes, the odours of tea and precious woods, the powerful aroma of opium and breaths heavy with perfumes ...

In this intoxication of reveries, debaucheries, tortures and crimes, it seemed as though all these mouths, all these hands and all these breasts, all this living flesh, were about to rush upon Clara to take pleasure with her dead body!

I was unable to move or say a word ... Near me, a young and pretty Chinese girl who was still a child with eyes that were both candid and lascivious, was displaying obscenely strange objects on a flat tray. There were shameless ivories, phalluses made of pink rubber and illumin-

151

ated books in which an artist's brush had reproduced the thousand complicated joys of love . . .

"Love! Love! Who wants love? I've got love for everybody!"

But I still bent over Clara once more.

"She must be brought to my room," ordered the Chinese girl with painted eyes.

Two strong men lifted the stretcher. I followed mechanically.

Led by the courtesan, we went down a vast corridor, as sumptuously decorated as a temple. To our left and our right, doors opened into large rooms with walls covered with hangings, lit with soft pink lights veiled in muslin . . . the thresholds were guarded with statues of symbolic animals with enormous, terrifying erect members and bisexual divinities prostituting themselves or straddling monsters in heat. Perfumes were burning in precious bronze vases.

A door-curtain of silk embroidered with flowers drew apart and revealed two women's heads. One of the women asked us as we passed:

"Who is dead?"

The other replied:

"But no one, of course! No one is dead. You can see that it's the woman of the Garden of Tortures . . ."

The name of Clara, whispered from lip to lip, from bed to bed and from room to room soon spread from one end of the boat to the other like some marvellous obscenity. It even seemed to me that the bronze monsters were repeating her name in their orgasms and shrieking it in their delirium of blood-stained lust.

"Clara! Clara! Clara!"

Here, I glimpsed a young man stretched out on a bed. The little lamp of an opium den was smouldering within reach of his hand. There was something like a painful ecstasy in his strangely dilated eyes . . . Before him, pressed mouth to mouth, breast to breast, hip to hip, naked women were entwined and dancing sacred dances while musicians kneeling behind a screen were playing their short flutes ... There, I saw other women sitting in circles or lying on mats on the floor in obscene poses, waiting with faces that were sadder with their lust than the faces of tortured victims. In front of every door we passed there were groans, panting voices, gestures of damned souls, twisted and crushed bodies and a whole world of grimacing pain which sometimes screamed under the lash of atrocious pleasures and barbaric onanisms. I saw a bronze group guarding one door and the mere arabesque of its lines made me thrill with horror ... It was an octopus entwining its tentacles around the body of a virgin and pumping love, the whole of love, from her mouth, her breasts and her womb with its ardent, powerful suckers ...

I thought I was in a house of torture rather than one of joy and love.

So crowded did the corridor become that for a few seconds we were obliged to stop before a chamber—the largest of them all—which differed from the others by its decorations and its sinister red lighting. At first, all I could see were women—a mêlée of frantic flesh and brightly coloured scarves—who were abandoning themselves to frenzied dances and fits of demoniacal possession around a kind of idol of massive bronze with ancient patina, standing in the centre of the room and towering up as high as the ceiling. Then I saw the Idol clearly and realised that it was that terrible Idol known as the Idol of the Seven Penises ... An enormous torso, or rather a single enormous belly set on a huge, phalliform, barbaric column, was crowned by three heads with red horns and writhing flames for hair. All around the column, at the precise spot where the monstrous belly ended, there protruded seven phalluses to which the dancing women were proffering flowers and furious endearments. The red glow in the

153

chamber gave the jade eyes of the Idol a diabolical semblance of life ... Just as we were about to continue, I witnessed an unspeakable sight, the infernal frenzy of which no words can describe. Seven shrieking, sobbing women all rushed upon the seven bronze phalluses, enlacing and straddling the Idol until it was violated by a mass of delirious flesh and quivered under the simultaneous shock of all these acts of possession and furious kisses which resounded like so many blows of a battering-ram upon the gates of some besieged city. All around the Idol there was a demented clamour, a delirium of savage voluptuousness and a writhing of bodies that were so frantically interlaced and conjoined that the scene took on the aspect of a massacre and reminded me of the murderous struggle of the prisoners in the iron cage as they fought over Clara's bit of rotten meat! In that one atrocious instant, I understood that lust can descend to the depths of human terror and give a true picture of hell and all its horrors ...

It seemed to me that all these savage shocks of human flesh, all these panting voices, groans and bites and even the Idol itself only knew one word to express their furious, unslaked lusts and their raging impotence :

"Clara! ... Clara! ... Clara! ..."

When we had reached the chamber and laid the still unconscious Clara on a bed, my senses returned to me and I realised where I was. All these songs, these debauches, sacrifices, nauseous perfumes and impure bodily contacts which were sullying the sleeping soul of my mistress inspired me not so much with horror as with an overwhelming shame. I had great trouble in dismissing the curious, chattering women who had followed us and in making them go away not only from the bed where we had laid Clara but even from the room. I only kept Ki-Pai with me for despite her grumpy airs and her rough words she showed herself to be greatly devoted to her mistress and showed great delicacy and skill as she tended her.

Clara's pulse was still beating with the same reassuring regularity as though she were in the full vigour of health. Not for a minute had life ceased to inhabit that body which seemed dead. Ki-Pai and I both bent anxiously over her, waiting for the first sign of resurrection.

All of a sudden, Clara uttered a low moan; the muscles of her face contracted and slight nervous tremors shook her bosom, arms and legs. Ki-Pai said :

"Now she will have a terrible crisis. We must hold her strongly and take care that she doesn't tear her face or her hair with her nails."

I thought that Clara could hear me and that if she knew I was with her her crisis would be soothed... I murmured in her ear, trying to fill my words with all the caresses of my voice, all the tenderness of my heart and all the pity—ah yes, all the pity!—on earth...

"Clara... Clara... it's me... Look at me... Listen to me..."

But Ki-Pai put her hand over my mouth.

"Be quiet!" she ordered imperiously, "how do you expect her to hear us? She's still with the evil spirits."

Then, Clara began to struggle. All her muscles began to tense and contract with frightful contortions... Her joints cracked like the rigging of a sailing ship in a storm... An expression of suffering whose horror was made even more horrible by her silence invaded her twisted face until it resembled that of the tortured man under the bell in the garden. All we could see of her eyes between the half-closed, fluttering eyelids, were a thin white line... Flecks of foam were bubbling on her lips. Panting, I asked Ki-Pai :

"My God! What will happen to her?"

She replied :

"Hold her down but leave her body free for the devils

must go from her body."

She then added :

"It's over . . . Now she will cry . . . "

We were holding her wrists to prevent her tearing her face with her nails. There was such strength in her that I thought she was going to dislocate our hands . . . In one last convulsion, her whole body arched, from her heels to her neck, and her tensed skin vibrated. Then, little by little, the crisis passed. Her muscles slackened back into their usual position and she slumped back on the bed, her eyes full of tears.

For a few minutes she wept and wept . . , tears ran down from her eyes silently as from a spring!

"It's over," said Ki-Pai, "now you can speak to her."

Clara's hand was now lying limp, damp and softly in my own. Her eyes were still glazed and remote as she tried to regain awareness of the objects and forms around her. She seemed to be coming out of some long, anguished sleep.

"Clara! My little Clara!" I murmured.

She gave me a long, sad, veiled look through her tears.

"You," she said. "You . . . ah yes!"

Her voice was barely a whisper.

"It is I! It is I! Clara, here I am! Do you recognise me?"

She laid her cheek against mine and beseeched me :

"Don't move . . . I'm all right like this . . . I'm pure like this . . . I'm all white . . . all white like an anemone!"

I asked her if she was still suffering.

"No, no! I'm not suffering . . . And I'm happy to be here, with you . . . so little and so near you . . . so little . . . so little . . . and all white . . . white as one of those little swallows in a Chinese fable . . . you know . . . those little swallows . . . "

All she said—she only barely whispered—were little words of purity and whiteness . . . From her lips there only came words like "little flowers", "little birds", "little stars" and "little streams" and "soul", "sky" and "sky" ...

Now and again she stopped her twittering to clutch my hand even more tightly and lean her cheek against mine.

"Oh, my darling," she said more firmly, "never again, I swear to you! Never again! Never again!"

Ki-Pai had withdrawn to a corner of the room and was softly singing a cradle song—a cradle song to send little children to sleep.

"Never again! Never ... never again!" said Clara slowly, in a soft voice that mingled with Ki-Pai's slow, soft singing.

She fell asleep against me ... A calm, luminous, remote sleep as tranquil as a great lake under a midsummer's night's moon.

Ki-Pai noiselessly stood up.

"I'm going!" she said. "I'm going to sleep in the sampan ... Tomorrow morning when dawn comes, you will take my mistress back to the palace ... And then it will all begin again ... It will always begin again!"

"Don't say that!" I beseeched her. "Look at her sleeping beside me! Look at her sleeping so purely and calmly!"

The Chinese woman nodded her head and with sad eyes in which pity had taken the place of disgust she said:

"I see her sleeping beside you and I say to you: in a week I shall be taking both of you, like tonight, on the river on your way back from the Garden of Tortures ... And years later, I shall still be taking you on the river if you have not gone away and if I am not dead!"

She added:

"And if am dead, another will take you on the river with my mistress. And if you are gone, then another will accompany my mistress on the river ... And nothing will have changed ... "

"Ki-Pai, why do you say that? Look again at her, while

157

she sleeps ! You don't know what you're saying !"

"Hush !" she said, laying a finger on her mouth. "Don't talk so loudly. Don't move so much ... Don't wake her ... At least, when she sleeps she does no evil, neither to herself nor to others !"

Carefully walking on tip-toe, like a nurse, she went towards the door and opened it.

"Go away ! Go away !"

Ki-Pai's voice was cutting imperiously through the humming chatter of the women outside. I saw painted eyes and faces, red mouths, tattooed breasts, lips pressed against breasts and heard cries, moans, dances and flutes, the thud of flesh against metal and that name that ran panting from mouth to mouth, like a spasm shaking the entire boat :

"Clara ! ... Clara ! ... Clara !"

The door shut again, the noises died away and the faces were gone.

I was alone in the room, where two lamps veiled with pink gauze were softly burning ... I was alone with Clara who was sleeping and muttering in her sleep like a tiny child dreaming :

"Never again ! ... Never again !"

As though to belie her words, a bronze monkey I had not seen before and which was squatting in the corner of the room, seemed to be pointing its erect monstrous member at Clara and sniggering ferociously.

Oh ! If only she would never, never wake again !

"Clara ! ... Clara ! ... Clara ! ..."¹